LINCOLN

THE MANNING DRAGONS BOOK 3

KATHI S. BARTON

This is a work of fiction. Names, characters, places, and incidents are products of the author's imagination or are used fictitiously and are not to be construed as real. Any resemblance to actual events, locations, organizations, or persons, living or dead, is entirely coincidental.

World Castle Publishing, LLC
Pensacola, Florida
Copyright © Kathi S. Barton 2018
Paperback ISBN: 9781629899213
eBook ISBN: 9781629899220
First Edition World Castle Publishing, LLC, April 16, 2018
http://www.worldcastlepublishing.com

Cover: Karen Fuller
Editor: Maxine Bringenberg

Table of Contents

Chapter 1

Lincoln looked at the bins being filled with food and the ice going into the meat display. It was finally here. The grand opening of the Greenhouse and Market Place, or GhMP for short. He loved it.

"Hey, Lincoln? You have a minute?" He said that he did for him. Ben was a good kid and had been there from the first. "Sure, you do. I think you've found out I'm the biggest pain in the ass here. But there are some veggies I wanted to ask you about. You said this stuff was from the warehouse? Well, I think they sent us the wrong stuff."

Looking it over, he wondered why he thought that until he saw the invoice on the top. This was for a store in Birmingham. Pulling out his cell phone, he called his buddy, Alex, to ask him about it. Alex Porter shipped fruits and vegetables all over the state of Ohio, and sometimes to others. And he was going to sell off his extra, sometimes damaged, things here in the marketplace. When the phone was answered, he asked to speak to Alex. When he came on the line, he explained what was going on.

"It's yours. The people declined their order for yesterday, and if you can take it off my hands, I'll give you half. There's an invoice that should be with it." He told Alex that there was. "Good. She's going to get charged for the entire invoice, so you can get what you can out of it. Her contract said that she got one chance at this and that's all. I don't want to have ripe fruits in my warehouse all week that'll be rotten before the end of today. I don't work that way. If you can sell it, I won't have wasted my money on bringing it back to the warehouse."

"I wouldn't even know how to price this, Alex. I know very little about fruit. And you know me, I don't bother with the stuff unless it's under threat of death. And don't get me started on vegetables."

Alex asked if Ben was there. Handing him the phone so they could work this out, he walked down the rest of the causeway to make sure all the booths were filled.

Lincoln could have occupied them several times over if need be. There was a waiting list about a mile long with names and products. When he saw his buddy from up north, the two of them embraced.

"I'm nervous." Peter told him he'd be too if this was his first day. "We went for a Monday morning on purpose. Sort of a soft opening. That way we can work out the kinks before the.... What are you laughing about?"

"Your soft opening is for shit, you know that, don't you?" He said that they weren't expecting a huge crowd. "Linc, when I drove up here, I had to wait in line twenty minutes to get into the parking lot. And that's not counting the line out front, just waiting for the doors to open. You're going to have a very busy soft opening."

"There's a lot of people?" He asked if he'd gotten banks for people in the event they needed cash. "Yes, just as you told — There really are that many here? We didn't even advertise so it would be a slow day. Which it won't be, will it? How many are out there, you think?"

"I'd say a few thousand." Lincoln nearly fell over. And might have but for Peter grabbing him. "Just stay focused and you'll be fine. Go tell your people to gear up, they're coming to see them in about four minutes."

Lincoln sprinted down the lines, and into the building, to tell them. Word had traveled fast. By the time he got to the last line of the six rows of vendors, they were already putting out more of their product. He was glad now that someone had suggested he call in some off-duty cops to help with the crowd. And banks for extra cash just in case. He'd have to tell Peter thanks.

"Have you seen the crowd out there?" He told Cooper not now. "I know, but you said that this was going to be a trial run, not all of the state — "

"Cooper, I don't think you're helping." Lincoln felt green when Carson asked if he needed anything. Then the sting to his cheek made him rub it while looking at her. "You're just lucky I hit you and not Winnie. Now, what do you need us to do? We're here for you."

"Take a row and see if they need anything after the first half hour. I have extra cash should they need it. I'll give you one to sell to each vendor. There is a thousand in each, all ones and fives." Cooper took his bag and the apron that said Marketplace on it.

By the time the gates were opened, the rest of his family had shown up. He gave them each an apron and a bag of cash. Before nine-thirty, half an hour after the gates opened, he was making another run to the bank. Thank goodness it was a weekday.

After about eleven, things started to slow down. Everyone he talked to while helping with the overload of customers was happy. Some said that they were never leaving. He was glad for that. And that he had taken the time to listen to everyone's advice. It would have been a disaster if he hadn't.

He'd been about to take out an ad in the local paper. Lincoln wanted things to go well for the vendors. But he'd been told if they were overwhelmed the first day, they might not come back. Most had never done anything like this before.

At noon, they got another wave of people. Businesswomen and men coming to check them out and grab some lunch. A lot of the restaurants were busy, and were also selling quite a few drinks. If this was what he could expect in May, he wondered what it could be like when the weather was hot. He'd cross that bridge when he came to it.

Ben joined him. "What do you want me to do?" He asked if he had a replacement at the fruit stand. "Nah, it's all gone. We even sold the boxes, believe it or not."

"What do you mean, it's all gone? There was a truckload, and I do mean that literally, of things there. Did you sell that too?"

"Yeah, your nephews came to help, Simon the most. We bagged and unloaded while the little one, John, pitched for me. You know, five oranges for five bucks kinda thing. You have yourself a nice barker there if you need him." He didn't think the kid would lie to him, but he went to check, just to assure himself. "I called Peter, and he said congrats. Also, that now he'll know to double up this weekend. And he made a hefty profit too. He's thrilled."

"Are you coming back?" He asked if Simon and John were going to help. "I can ask their parents, but I think they're here already. How long did they work? I'll need to make sure they're paid."

"Peter said he'd take care of them. I turned their hours in with mine. I was told to do it that way, Mr. Manning." He wasn't sure that he was going to agree to that but said nothing to the young man. "Also, Mr. Pack, the meat guy, fed us with his employees. Said he was having such a great day that he didn't mind whatsoever."

Lincoln went to find Cooper and Carson to tell them the kids had done a good job. They were at the meat counter themselves, and Mr. Pack was telling him what a great day he'd had. He wanted to know if there was going to be a permanent place for him. Lincoln told him that all the inside vendors were welcome to sign a lease for their space after next week. Lincoln didn't want anyone to feel like they'd made a mistake.

"I didn't by coming here. No siree, I'm telling you, son, I did more business today than in a month at my location. The parking is better, and people feel safer here because you have it all lit up. You did good, Lincoln. I'll be here for as long as you'll let me."

The man selling cookies looked as if he'd closed early, but

in actuality had sold nearly every cookie and cupcake he'd brought. So, he was talking to the customers walking around and telling them he'd have more when he opened Wednesday.

Everyone that he and Cooper had spoken to as they went around collecting their views on how it went today didn't have one thing bad to say. Most had sold out before lunch, and the rest had been close to that. Even the spice guy said he'd had one of the best days ever. Cooper said that he'd bought a few things as well.

"It was fun because of all the people here. Most of them were in such high spirits that it was difficult to be upset about a few extra minutes in a line." He laughed. "You'll need to have the port-a-john people come out more often if this is the trend here."

At midnight he was still in his office. Today's sales were through the roof if the totals were correct. Everyone had given him their daily total so that he could go to the bank when the month was out and apply for an expansion on the land he'd already had. There were another fifteen acres where he was going to add some outdoor activities for the kids, as well as weekend vendors that sold their own art.

He was just putting things away for the night when Ginger Rice came to see him. "I heard you had a good day." He smiled and told her he'd had a fantastic one. "Good. Can you use some help with the bookkeeping? I have Cooper all settled in, and since I can do it daily now instead of catching him up, I have some spare time on my hands."

"Your sister comes tomorrow, doesn't she? I heard she's met Garrett and he sort of overwhelmed her a little." She smiled and said that she was cursing like a sailor. "I'm really glad that he could help her. And yes, if you have time, I'd love for you to handle that. I have an idea what to do, but I'd be slow in learning it."

"Grace will take up some of my time, but she wants to make sure Walton isn't going to bother us anymore. She's hated him from the very beginning. And I'm to understand that the other day he found out I had a son, not a daughter." He asked how that went over when she stood. "I wish he'd not found out until after the trial, but I really don't care. He tried to have me, and my children, killed, and he isn't getting me back for any amount of money or begging. I'm done with his ass."

"Your happy with your house and children being around? I mean, I know it's sort of big, but as a rental, it's all right. Cooper has owned it for some time, I'm to understand." She said that she was very happy with her living arrangements. "Good. Family is both good and bad at times. I'm so thankful you are the former."

"Are you saying you don't care for yours?" He laughed and said that he loved them very much. "Then I don't understand. I thought you guys were all very close."

"Oh, we are. Very much so. And that is the problem." She said that she understood now. When her faerie joined them in the room, Lincoln could see that she was happy with her too. Lincoln had his own, Drizzle, and he found the little man to be quite useful. "I'll take off now and come by sometime tomorrow. I'm to understand that after today, you won't be open on Mondays, correct?"

"You are. We took a vote, the tenants and I, and we all decided that Monday, after a long weekend, will be just be

11

the perfect day to rest and stock up. I'm not sure what we're doing for the Fourth just yet, but we'll get to that soon." She said that it was only six weeks away. "I know. Spring has just flown by, don't you think?"

"It has." She looked around the office. "You're going to need some supplies in here for me to work. I'll need only a few things that I can bring from my office."

"Order what you need, and I'll pick it up at the stationary store for you. I'll also set up an account like my brother has. Cooper said that he's never had it so easy before." She told him they were making her life better. "All the same, you're a welcome treat to have around. Even if you weren't a wizard at bookkeeping."

After making her list, she talked to him while he finished what he had to do. She said she'd come in Monday when it would be quiet in the office. He told her that a lot of people were going to come in and do restocking, so she might want to barricade herself in the office. She laughed at that.

"I'll let them in if you make it so I know them. I don't want to let in shoppers or some robber while I'm here." He told her that he'd put a lock on the doors that they had to have a badge to get in with. "That's very clever. My goodness, you Mannings sure do have a lot of experience in this, I guess."

"We've been around for a long time."

Ginger left after they talked for a bit. He could tell that she was excited about her sister coming while also dreading it. She sounded a little on the caustic side, and he had a feeling she was going to be his mate.

Lincoln didn't know why though. Probably because he was too busy to woo a woman, and Grace sounded like she was so far opposite of him that it sometimes made him want to crawl into a deep cave and make himself a hermit when he thought about her. But he liked people too much to do that.

At one o'clock he left his office at the greenhouse. Tomorrow they were going to be open, but he both hoped and didn't that they had another like today. The greenhouse had had a good day too, selling all the planters as well as taking orders for more. He had a feeling that the weekend before the Fourth they were going to be really busy, due to people getting their houses ready for the big day.

His house was beginning to fill out. Having the funds to have all the renovations done the way he wanted them was nice. But he was sick of having workers around all the time. Davie, the contractor, said they'd be done this coming week, and he was looking forward to it. The only rooms complete were his bedroom and the kitchen.

Tomorrow was a big day and he was going to enjoy it. There were too many things going on in his head for him to sleep, so he went for a walk. The moon was just bright enough to light his way. Lincoln loved the solitude of the woods and the bewitching hour. He also knew that he'd sleep better after a good stretch.

~~~

Grace wasn't happy. Firstly, she felt like she was being ambushed. Secondly...well, she was pissed off. She wasn't even sure at what just yet, but she was all the same. When the man in charge of her feeling this way came toward her, she put up her hand.

"You know that you can't keep me away. I just came to tell you that you've sold another painting." She looked at him

13

with a stern eye. "You can glare all you want, but I did tell you that you'd have a good showing."

"It's not even until tonight. How are these people—? You're letting some come in now?" He said that they were his patrons. "I don't care if they're your brothers, you said that I'd have a good show tonight. I'm not prepared for this."

"That's why you have me." She could honestly say that she could gladly kill Garrett Massey and whoever had told him about her. If it was Ginger, she was going to murder her too. "There are things going on in your head that are very frightening, aren't they?"

"I'm planning your demise." He laughed. The man was forever doing that. "What do I do if there isn't anything left to sell? Not that I think that's going to happen. But do you have a backup plan if it does?"

"Yes, talk you into the other twelve paintings that you have stashed in my office. You let me put them out and we'll have an even better showing." She said that she didn't care anymore. "Seriously? Great. I have just enough time to display them. And since you don't want to know what I'm selling them for, you're going to be pleasantly surprised, I think."

"I don't know how you sold the first one, much less two. Those prices are well above what I would have sold them for, aren't they?" He said again that was why she had him. "I don't know what's going on. What if these people get home and say they don't like them? Are you going to make me give you the money back?"

"I don't think anyone is going to do that. And they sign a contract when they buy a piece of work from here; it's theirs. You worry too much, sweetie." He laughed again, and she

14

wanted to punch him. Twice. "Besides, I doubt very much that once your name gets out there, anyone will want to return them. You'll be a hit, and those first pieces will be worth a great deal more than they are right now."

"They're not worth the price you're putting on them. I don't know how much, but I know it's more than I would have charged. Also, I can't believe people are going to pay you whatever you want for my work. It's insane." He kissed her on the forehead and she stood there when he walked away. She wanted her sister.

Grace wasn't one to whine and complain. She was more the type of person that took care of things when they came up, and usually with flare. At least that's what she called it. Her flare was to ignore the person causing her issues. Or—and it amazed her how many times this plan came up—she kicked the shit out of them. Pulling out her cell, she called her sister.

"I was wondering if you'd call." Grace felt better just hearing her voice. "I just laid Mattie down for a nap and I'm feeding Wendall, so you can talk to me all you want."

"You're so domestic. I miss that about you." Her sister laughed and told her she could be too. "No way. I don't like people. I called to see if you're still going to make it tonight. You're my rock."

"I am. I have the best sitter ever keeping an eye on the children, and I have this dress that is going to make you jealous." She hadn't told her sister that she'd had a makeover and felt foolish in her own. "All of the Mannings are coming too. You're going to be overwhelmed, all right. Just don't hit any of them."

"I don't hit people right off the bat." She laughed with

15

Ginger. "I've warned Garrett we're twins and it's difficult to tell us apart. Hopefully everyone will think you're the artist and leave me alone."

"And what would I say if they were to ask about a piece? Nothing. I wouldn't even know what to tell them about the kind of paint you use. Besides, you'll be just fine." Ginger told her to hang on. "I had to switch boobs."

"You don't need to tell me that." She did though, and it was great that her sister was so happy. "I've hired this guy to take care of my work. Though I don't think there was ever a doubt to him that he was. He seems to think that I'm the best thing since sliced bread. And that's what he said to me. And he's a tiger."

"Yes, I know that. The men here, they have all kinds of paranormals coming in and out all the time. I'm getting good at telling the difference. Oh, and I took on another client. I'll be doing Lincoln's books now too. I'm having so much fun." She told her only she would have fun with numbers. "They sing their song to me. And you should know how that is. You tell me all the time how your muse seems to call to you. Does he still zone you out when you paint, like he did all the time?"

"Yeah, I'm weird like that." She saw Garrett pulling her paintings out to the floor. "I have to go and see what he's about. I gave him the last of twelve to put out for tonight. I think I'll be bringing them when I come see you."

She wanted to bring her sister home with her, to her house, but she didn't have that anymore. As soon as she told her landlord she was going away for an extended period, he told her that he was selling the house and she might as well move out. It was very abrupt, but she knew it was coming.

16

He was ninety-two and had no one to help him with rentals anymore.

"I had to sell, honey. I loved you being here all the time, but I'm falling more and more, and I can't be doing that and living by myself. I got into one of the assisted living places. They'll even do my clothes for me. Imagine that, why don't you, somebody to wash my undies." They laughed. "I'll give you back your deposit, and you can take your time moving out. I'm sorry."

She and Ginger talked about this and that when they were on the phone nowadays. It was comforting because Ginger was so calm. They talked mostly about the children, who Grace was excited to see. Mattie had been just a wee thing the last time she'd seen her, and now there was a little boy. Ginger deserved so much better than the ass that had taken her.

"I have to go, sweetie. We need to get dressed up, and I should do that now while Wendall and Mattie are asleep. I'll see you tonight and you'll be coming with us." She said that she hoped she could find a place to live. "You will. You can live with us. We'll have good times again."

After hanging up, she went to the office to see what was left. Really, it was to hide out. She really wasn't very good with people. They made her freeze up. She thought that was why she painted, just to escape the world.

Last night, it had taken her an hour tossing and turning to realize she wasn't going to sleep. So instead of continuing down that futile path, she got up and pulled out her things. The hotel she was staying at, thanks to Garrett, said she could paint in her room but would be responsible for any damage done to it. Garrett had put down a large deposit and told her that he'd pay for any damages. To paint when the mood struck her was something she couldn't do without. It, like her sister and her children, calmed her in ways she couldn't explain. Last night's painting had been the best she thought she'd ever done.

For some reason the idea of a large castle had come to her. Not the pretty kind with turrets with flags and flowers at the front. This one was dark and full of secrets that only the ghosts that lived there were aware of. And they were going to keep out everyone that tried to come to the big stack of stone. As she painted, seeing it in her mind's eye, she got more information on the inhabitants there, and was glad for the lights when the darkness of the place started to make itself known to her.

Death was all over it. It had been in a siege and many lives were lost. The king had killed his wife, to save her from certain death that would not be easy on the delicate lady. Then he'd thrown himself out the window, sure that it would be preferable than the one the new king would have for him. There were other stories like that one, but she loved rather than hated them.

Part of the castle wasn't coming to her, but she was all right with that. Instead of trying to make it, she just painted something else on it. The broken gates, the large stones at intervals around the place. There were other things that had fallen into disrepair, but she had a feeling the castle and its surroundings were going to be something that would haunt her forever. Like the unfinished part of the castle, something was blocking her from seeing it all.

When she stepped back from it when her alarm went off to get up, she was amazed at the detail. But then she was like that with each of her paintings. But in this one, this was calling to her in a different way. Like *she* had the unfinished business, not the castle. Cleaning up, she noticed something that she hadn't before. The makings of a dragon that seemed to be flying over the castle, the part that she'd not finished. Seemingly protecting it from whatever was coming for it. Or her.

"What is wrong with you?" she had asked herself. "It's a painting, not a fortune teller. Get a grip, dumbass."

And now here she sat, wanting to work on it, but knowing that for now it was as finished as she could make it. Until... whatever was needed for her to do was ready. Laughing to herself, she decided to return to the hotel anyway and get dressed. Tonight was going to be huge for her, and she'd get to see her sister.

Taking a second shower, Grace pulled her hair into a ponytail and then braided it. After wrapping it with a rubber band, she coiled it around her head, mostly to keep it out of her face. Then she pulled her dress on. Black, Garrett had told her — to show how important she was. Instead she felt foolish. She never wore dresses at all, and this was strange.

It was more of a sheath, she supposed. There wasn't any kind of nipping at the waist. The only part that was tight was around her breasts. And there was a slit up the side that showed off her entire leg and most of her thigh. She wasn't thrilled about that, but it was the only dress they had in her size that was black. She was going to have to do some serious shopping if she had to do this very often. Grace did not like showing off more than she saw in her mirror every day.

Chapter 2

Lincoln was getting dressed when his brother contacted him. Tristan was having trouble with his tux and wondered if Lincoln could please help him. He asked what the problem was. Tristan said he was coming over.

The doorbell rang just a few minutes later, which told him that his brother had been on his way. As soon as he opened the door, he could see what was wrong. He had no idea how to make his tie work. Pulling him into the hallway, Lincoln had him set in seconds. His butler, Milton, met them at the front door with their capes. They were going all out on this thing, it appeared.

"I don't want to be a caped crusader." Milton simply cleared his throat, standing there holding them out as if he'd not said a word. "You do know that you work for me, not the other way around?"

"Lady Carson said if you gave me any trouble, I was to call her. This is the sister to one of our own, she said I was to tell you, and you were to behave, or she'd make you hurt." He looked at them. "She is scary when she wants something, is she not?"

"She is at that. So is Winnie. And she's the one that would make me hurt in ways I don't even want to think about." They all laughed as Lincoln and Tristan pulled on the capes. He had to admit, they did make a striking pair. Tristan continued speaking as they headed out. "I've been talking to Ginger about her sister, and I just know she's my mate. She's going to have me for dinner. I don't do well with aggressive women."

"You'll do fine. It's funny, Xavier and I have been saying the same thing about her being mated to one of us." Tristan told him Lucas was bored with the whole thing of finding a mate. "Is he now? Then I hope its him. He deserves to be with the ball buster."

"Who's a ball buster?" The limo had pulled up as he was saying that, and Carson had, of course, heard him. "You mean me? Then I thank you. I love that I can stand my own ground. And I'm glad to see that you didn't give poor Milton any trouble about the capes. He's a nice man to put up with you."

"You are one, but we were referring to Grace." Ginger laughed then, and he smiled at the pretty woman. "She is going to bust our balls, isn't she?"

"Oh yes, you can bet on it. And I hope one of you are going to be her mate. It would be perfect for her to have someone like you guys in her corner." He asked what she meant. "For all her ball busting, as you called it, Grace is more tender than I am. She just hides it better with violence and mayhem. I don't know if she still does it or not, but when she was drawing when were kids, she'd sob after she was finished, because it was the last one, she would tell me. And she had some trouble with a few people she worked with at the plant. I don't know all of it, but she's been hurt before. They don't like having a woman boss."

"What does she do there? We have the distribution plant here. Perhaps she can shed some light on smaller issues we've been having." Ginger told Cooper she'd find it. "Good. Even though it's running now, there are still points we could use help on."

"Grace was the manager of the entire place. And she did a great job too. They were having some major shrink issues and she found them and cut them out. They're down to less than one percent now where they had been at eighteen." Carson asked what had happened with the trouble that she'd had. "I don't know. She's very private, even with me. But I know that she gave notice about a month ago. I don't know what went down, but she's less stressed about everything now. She told me today she'll need to find a place to live around here. I'm hoping that means she's going to stay. I've missed her."

Lincoln could understand that. He saw his brothers every day and didn't know what it would be like to have one so far away. Even if they were only in the next state, he'd reach out, talk through his day with them. And if he didn't, they would him. It was what they had always done, be there for each other.

They were pulling up in front of the gallery when he realized they were going to be spending the night in town, and he had no place arranged. Oh well. And he'd have to go shopping as soon as possible to get something to wear home.

Either that, or he'd be the butt end of every joke they could manage from wearing his tux home when they all had jeans and T-shirts, he'd bet.

The first thing he saw when he entered was the art on the main wall, and it blew him away. The painting was called Evening Train. He loved how the locomotive seemed to jump right off the canvas at him. Almost as if he should move out of the way or be run down. But the subtleties were what got him. The man standing on the tracks as the train came at him. The happy face of the person in the front cab, who hadn't noticed the other man. There was a stream of smoke coming out the top that made him think of how fast it seemed to be going. There was a sad feeling about it, and he wondered if that was what she'd meant to do.

Lincoln looked in the direction Ginger was when she said her sister was there. He couldn't see her yet, but he could feel his dragon stirring. Looking around for whatever was making him nervous, he started toward them when he saw Garrett. It was him that was in trouble; not really, but he was nervous about something. Lincoln didn't know why yet, but he went to see if he could help him.

"What do you think of the artist?" He told Garrett he'd not met her yet. "She's going to flip out when the night is over. She has it in her head that nothing is going to sell. But I have a feeling she's going to have people begging for more of her work."

"Speaking of which, I want the train one in the front." He told him that it was sold. "Damn. That is a wonderful painting. It says a great deal, doesn't it?"

"I didn't get it until she showed me. The man on the

tracks? I never saw it. Nor the other things on the painting." He asked if he meant the note in his hands. "Yes, as you can well imagine, I felt foolish. But like you, I fell in love with it. To be honest, Lincoln, she wasn't going to let me show it. I had to almost beg her to release the others in the room. It has me a little nervous, if you want the truth. I think she's going to outgrow me before this thing even starts to make either of us some serious money."

They wandered around the gallery, pointing out which were sold and the ones he thought would go next. He loved the train though, that was his favorite, but the woman had talent, he could see that.

Ginger was coming toward them when he saw the woman. Christ, she was a dream, which was weird to say considering she and Ginger were twins. And to say that she looked like Ginger would have been an understatement. They were identical. Even their dresses, one blue, the other black, made them seem more alike. He moved toward her when Ginger said his name.

"Lincoln, I'd like you to meet my sister, Grace. Grace, this is the man I was telling you about, Lincoln Manning, who opened the greenhouse marketplace." He heard her talking, Ginger was, but he only had eyes for Grace. And he knew as soon as he touched her what she was to him.

"You're holding me too tight." When he let her go, Grace glared. "What the fuck is wrong with you? Surely, you've seen a woman before tonight. And I would think you'd know not to manhandle them."

"I've never seen a woman like you." He knew he was messing this up and tried to regroup. "I'm terribly sorry. It's

25

been a long week, and I still have the weekend to go through. The greenhouse has been taking up a great deal of my time. If you could forgive me, we can start again. I'm Lincoln Manning. And yes, I know better than to manhandle women."

He looked for someone to get him out of this mess before he screwed up more. He needed someone to rescue him from himself. But Grace was called away and he let out a long breath. But he'd forgotten about Ginger, who was currently staring at him like he was a freak show.

"She belongs to you, doesn't she?" Lincoln told her that saying it like that to Grace might not go over well. "No, not with her it wouldn't. I'm happy for you, I really am, but she's not going to come easy. You are aware of that, aren't you?"

"Yes. I don't know what to tell her either. I mean, she doesn't strike me to be anything like you in how well you took what we were." She laughed and told him he was in big trouble. "Yes, I think you might be right on that. Please don't say anything to anyone just yet. I don't want her to find out from them before I can talk to her."

"I can do that. But she's far from stupid, and she knows what you are. Not all of it, but that you're all dragons." He nodded and thanked her for that. "Don't thank me yet. I love Grace, she's all I had in the world for a long time. Then when Maddie came along, we sort of drifted apart. But when I was having trouble with Walton, she wasn't just there for me, but gave me money I'm sure she didn't have to help me get away. Then he tried to kill us."

"I'll be careful with her. Do you think she'll do the same for me?" Ginger just laughed as she walked away. "I'm so fucked right now."

He moved around the gallery again, this time looking for a painting that didn't have a blue sticker on the name. It looked as if she was having a good show if those were any indication. Lincoln found Grace in one of the back rooms staring at a painting entitled simply Mine.

"This one is dark too. Are all your paintings that way with a secondary meaning?" She glanced at him, then back at the painting. He wasn't even sure if she was going to answer, but she finally did.

"I live in a dark place when I paint. Most of the time, when I need to step back from them, I'm amazed at what I've done. I sort of zone out." He stood closer to get a better look at the canvas and see if he could touch her. "I'm painting one now, in my hotel room, that looks like I'm going to be in trouble before it's finished."

"Why would you say that?" Lincoln wanted to know how to protect her. How to make the painting be one of happiness instead of the dark he knew was going to be there. "Is someone threatening you?"

"Not at the moment. I might be soon, but not right now." She looked at him. "I got this burst of magic when we touched. It kind of freaked me out. Then when I was helping with the painting that this guy just had to have, I realized what it meant." He waited, not wanting her to know just yet, not until he was ready and wanting her to know so they could talk about it. Lincoln had never been so indecisive before. So, he changed the subject.

"I own this piece of land. It's a lot of acreage, but I'm happy with it. There were some things left in the house. Not a great many things—I'm guessing they were things they couldn't take when the house was emptied." Grace asked how many acres he had. "With the house, just over sixteen hundred. It's a lot. The second house, it came with a hundred, which we didn't know until the surveyor came out to do the job. There are also some buildings. A big metal one that someone took the time to mostly insulate and never used that I could see or smell. A regular barn, made of wood, that has the most amazing features to it. A water wheel that supplies the corn mill inside of it. Also, some of the land is rented by farmers who pay each year to have extras planted for their farms. I had no problem with it, so we're going to keep doing that."

"I lived in a rental house for most of my time out west. I hated it—being out west, not the house. But the landlord is retiring and has sold my house. Lucky for me he's a nice guy, and put all my things in storage." Lincoln said that was nice. "Yes. Are you nice, Lincoln? I'm not. I don't like people, and I'm hard on men. I want you to know that right up front. I'm not a pushover, and I don't jump when someone tells me to. Unless it's to keep me safe. I'm not that stubborn or stupid."

"I'm not good with people, but I like them. Mostly I avoid them because I'm never sure what to say when they ask a question." She nodded, and he turned to look at her. "I want you to like the house I bought. It's not necessary—I can sell it as it sits for more than I paid for it."

"I'm sure that it'll be fine." She laughed. "I never thought I'd be this calm about finding someone that was going to take over my life."

"I won't." She frowned and asked what he meant. "I won't take over your life. I can promise you that. I would like to be a part of it, in decisions you might make that would affect us both, but I will never tell you what to do nor how you should do it. And I'll do the same for you, not make any decisions that might alter how we do things."

"Ginger was hurt by a man. Twice as a matter of fact. She was married to Mattie's father for about a year and a half, and I guess the entire time he would beat her almost daily. She didn't try to get away from him. I think that was due to having Mattie and her being so young. She wanted it to make it work. He had money, you see, and Ginger didn't." He said he had money as well. "I know. Ginger told me that all of you have a great deal. But about the men in her life. Our parents were about as close as a jackal and a mouse to us. They were cold, and we figured out they didn't want us in their lives. I think that's why I'm so mean now. But one night, when we were sixteen, I'd had enough and packed us both up and we went to live with our Aunt Bev. She's a trip. Anyway, without her, I'm thinking that we might not have survived living on the streets. And that is why neither of us have been with another man since then that's been good to us. Walton, he didn't come into my sister's life, he sort of barged his way in and took over. I'm glad that he's no longer a threat to her."

"I will never harm you if I can help it. I have no desire to order you around. I want — no, that's not right. I need to make you happy, and I will try my very best to do so." She looked at the painting again. "And if you could paint me something like the train in the front, I'll be your slave for the rest of my life."

Her laughter made him smile. It might not be so bad having a mate that was sort of mean if she was like this. But he knew it wasn't something that he should count on. She had a temper, and Lincoln thought he might enjoy seeing it burn. So long as it wasn't aimed at him.

~~~

Walton looked up when he realized someone was with him. He'd seen people in and out of the area he was in all day. No one had come to visit, and for that he was pissed. He'd fucked up last night and was told his privileges were taken away. So, if anyone did come, they'd be refused. Though he had no idea who would want to see him. Ginger sure wouldn't.

What was wrong with that woman that she had to lie to him? He'd only wanted a son from her. A pretty woman like her, she should have been thrilled that a man like him would set his sights on her. He wasn't stupid—Walton had an education. He even had some cash stashed away he could have used. Or he could just go and take it from his father—now there was a person who had money. But Ginger and her kid were putting a drain on him, and he'd had enough. Especially after thinking he was going to have a daughter and not a son like he wanted. Why couldn't she just have had a boy? Then things would have been fine with them.

"Are you Walton George Conrad?" He said that he was but looked around when his middle name was put out there. "Are you? I'm looking for Walton George Conrad."

"Do you think you could forget my middle name, buddy? I hate it as much as I hate being in here." He stood and asked him what he wanted. "You're not a visitor, that much I can see."

"Here you go." He took the blue envelope—really, he'd had no choice—and the guy asked him to sign for it. "You don't have to. It's all right here on the camera on my chest,

30

as well as the one they have hanging out here, that you were served."

"Served? As in someone is trying to sue me? Who would do that?" He said that he didn't know, he'd have to read it. "Damn it all to hell and back. This had better not be my landlord again. I'll kick his ass."

It wasn't him, but Ginger suing him for child support. For his own kid. The paperwork even said how much he had stashed, as well as the value of the house they'd lived in. He couldn't understand how she'd know that unless....

"She went snooping around my things. How many times did I tell her to stay out of my boxes?" Walton sat on his bed and looked over the paperwork. "Oh no. Oh hell no, she is not hoping I'll pay for her daughter too? I'm not paying for that thief at all. I'd have a dragon but for her skinny little ass. All she had to do was leave my things alone, and that included my dragon. Then what does she do? She takes it out of the barn and steals it."

By the time dinner was served—another red-letter day in the meals this place handed out—he was seething mad at what she wanted from him. Walton was going to kill her as soon as he was free, and that kid too. And he would as soon as his attorney was aware of a few things. Like he'd fathered a son, not a daughter. And that she was trying to make it so he'd never see the kid. It was his, wasn't it?

There couldn't be any other way it would be someone else's. He'd fucked her every day until she got pregnant. He'd only let her go from the chain when he had to take her to the doctor, and even then, he'd made sure that she knew if she ran or told anyone, he'd kill the brat of hers.

31

Then she'd gone to the doctor and had them lie to him too. Telling him that she was carrying another girl and wasn't he so happy. Another little precious girl to raise.

"No, I was not. A little girl isn't at all what I wanted." He wasn't sure why that was so important, but that's what his father had always told him. Have a son, make sure there is someone to carry on the Conrad name. Like it was something to be proud of.

He supposed to his father it was. A rich fuck that had it all in a nice neat row. And he was tight too. Only gave Walton cash when he begged for it or made promises he wasn't going to keep. Like not coming home again. It was his fucking house too, wasn't it? His father had a screwed-up way of thinking when it came to him.

Now he was in jail for trying to kill her. If that other bitch had stayed out of his way, then he'd have no one but himself again. Women were the ruination of the world, his father used to say, and he was beginning to see that he might have been correct. They were only good for one single thing — well, two. Fucking and breeding sons.

Then there was the dragon. He'd caught it fair and square. Smiling to himself, he knew that was a fat lie too. He'd no more believed in them than he did faeries or unicorns. But he'd been at his buddy's house and he'd had him tied down with chains in his big barn that he told him had to be iron so he'd not get away.

It had taken him a great deal of planning to steal the dragon. It hurt him, too, that he'd had to end up killing his buddy over it. But when he found out that it could practically shit out money, he had to have it. There was never a time when you could have too much cash. And once he started reading up on them, the more he realized what the sucker was worth. Like every piece was worth millions. He had planned to start cutting away at the thing when he got rid of the kids and their mom. Then this had happened.

His trial date was set for next week. Walton had called his father, who in turn had gotten him a lawyer. Dad hadn't been that good of a role model for him, but when the shit hit the fan, like it had now, he could be counted on to help. He'd give you a hard time about it, but he'd get you to safer grounds.

"Mr. Conrad, you have a visitor. Now I'm going to let you see him today, but you explain that he can't come back tomorrow. You're grounded." He pointed out that he wasn't ten. "Then how about I tell that daddy of yours how you fucked up yesterday, and he'll just have to go back to where he came from?"

"I'll tell him." It wouldn't do any good. Telling his dad that he couldn't do something was the same as saying go right on ahead and do whatever it is you want. Just make sure you stayed out of his way. Dad was a force that no one screwed with. "If I'm still grounded, why am I seeing him? Not that I don't appreciate it?"

"You were served, and he said he was getting you an attorney. I can't deny you that." He nodded. "Also, he gave me some cash, and that gets you both a freebie."

Shuffling out to the area where he was allowed to see people, with chains on his ankles and wrists, he wasn't surprised all that much when he was led to a different place. One with a table and chairs, as well as food for him. Instead of eating it while the guard was in the room, he waited until his father dismissed him before reaching for the knife and fork. But before he could eat, the tray was shoved to the floor.

"You got caught, dummy. How many times have I told you to keep what you do at home behind your own closed doors? I said that to you every darned day, and now look where you are. I'm going to have to keep greasing palms, so you can get out and take care of business. What the F were you thinking?" His father rarely used the word fuck, replacing it with just the first letter when he was really pissed off. "Where is this woman that you knocked around?"

"I don't know. Isn't she at home?" He thought of something that would make his dad happy. "I have a son, dad. A little boy. I'm going to name him George Walton, after you." He wasn't, but Dad didn't have to know that right away.

"I thought you said she was having a girl." He said that she'd lied. "Women. That's all they do. Where is the boy? I'll get him and take him back with me."

There was something there that made him think as soon as he got his grandson, his father would wash his hands of him. But instead of saying again that he didn't know, he changed the subject.

"I was served. She wants me to pay child support for taking care of my own kid. Why would I have to when I could just take him from her and raise him myself? Maybe I'll have her pay me to watch over him." Father said that he'd take care of that. "I hope so. If she needs support, why doesn't she just drop this whole thing and give him to me? That way she won't be burdened."

"You won't be able to get him if she didn't put your name on the birth certificate. And I'll check into that as well.

Also, with having a criminal record and all the other shit that you've done since you were born, it'll be very hard to fight something you've been arrested for before. If that's the case, then you might not stand a chance in taking him. But I will. That's the way it should be anyway. I'm better equipped to handle him. If you go to prison, you can know he's in good hands." He asked if he was going to try and get him out. "Of course. I'd not let you rot in here. Though this is where you belong for getting caught with the goods, so to speak. I don't know who the person is that had you arrested, but she has some big balls to turn against my son. A grandson. I can't believe it; after all this time you finally did something right."

"I do things right all the time. You just choose not to notice them." His father just nodded. "I do. Who enlarged your dope area? I did. Who is the one that told you the building you wanted downtown was going up for sale?"

"Yes, and I didn't get that either, did I? Sometimes you're more trouble than you're worth. I blame it on your mother, God rest her soul." He pointed out that she wasn't dead. "She might as well be. And would be too, if she didn't have a pre-nup that I should never have signed, and then she wouldn't change everything over to me. I should never have let her live, that's all. Damn it all. I have a son."

"I do. You have a grandson."

Again, he was waved off, but it got him thinking. He wasn't getting out of here. Also, no matter what his father said, he wasn't going to take his son from him. Instead of listening, Walton started making his own plans. Not just to get out of here, but to get the boy too. And he'd kill whoever got in his way, including his own father. He'd fathered the boy, and he wanted to raise him. Bullshit on child support to Ginger. He would be the one getting paid.

Chapter 3

Grace was in shock. Garrett had taken her into his office when the show was still going on and told her she'd sold all but one of her paintings. Twice now she'd had to put her head between her knees, which wasn't easy with her dress, in order to not pass out. Sold all but one? How was that even possible?

"You want me to get someone for you?" The first person to pop into her head wasn't her sister, but Lincoln. Which was silly—she didn't even know him that well. "I can get Ginger for you, she's not too far away."

"Away? Did she leave?" He told her what she was doing. "Oh. She told me that she'd have to pump tonight. No, don't bother her. Could you maybe get one of the Mannings? I had a nice talk with the really tall one."

"They're all really tall, darling. But I'll get Lincoln since I know he's your mate." She didn't get a chance to ask how he knew because he was gone that fast. When the door opened again, she didn't even bother looking, knowing he'd turned her down.

"You can bring in one of the women then. I know it was a longshot to ask him in here." He cleared his throat and she turned to look at the most handsome man she'd ever laid eyes on. "I didn't think you'd come."

"Yes, well, he said you were hyperventilating, and needed someone to pick your chin up off the floor." She was going to kill Garrett. "You look better than I expected, at least. Are you all right? You don't look comfortable. Want me to hold your hand?"

"No, I'm not all right. I sold all but one of the paintings." He said that he'd heard and congratulated her. "I don't want to sell them all. I'm not that good."

"Apparently other people have a different opinion. Just so you know, I have the same one. You're very talented. And Ginger said you were self-taught. I'm very impressed with your work, honey." He sat down on the floor in front of her, and all she could think about was the color of his eyes. They were the most gorgeous shade of green that she'd ever seen. "How you doing now?"

She straightened, then stood when her dress started to ride up on her hips. He laughed when she struggled to pull it back into place. Grace didn't know whether to kick him or beg him to help her. Actually, she wanted him to remove it, and that thought tripped her up a little.

"I don't wear this kind of clothing often. Not ever, really, but Garrett told me I needed to make a statement. I didn't have any idea what I was supposed to be saying with the message, so I went with black like he suggested."

"Would you like to know what I think your statement is?"

She wasn't sure but nodded anyway. "I'm a powerful woman who knows her own worth. I'm sexy and I don't need to cover myself when in a man's world. I think with your talent, there will be men all over the world doubting they're really any good when compared to you."

"All over the world, huh? I doubt very much if anyone will care about this self-taught wannabe." He asked why she was a wannabe. "I have always wanted to be this premier artist. Painting wasn't my first choice, but it went much better than being a potter or even someone that sewed. Which I failed at both big time but would honestly like to try again. And then one afternoon, while I was putting my paints away, the gas man was reading the meters and asked if I'd sell him the one he'd seen in the kitchen. I don't even remember now how much he paid me, but it wasn't a lot."

"He's going to be jumping for joy when it gets out that you are a premier artist. I think anyone that has one of your paintings will be selling them soon enough." She laughed. "I'm serious. You're that good."

"I'm average at best. And don't get me wrong—I'm not fishing for compliments, I just know what I do and how good I am at it. And it's fun. I don't want it to ever become something that I need to do to make money. I think that would take all the joy out of it." He asked her about the painting in the hotel room. "It's not finished."

She was embarrassed to tell anyone about it. Especially this man. A dragon. She must have been thinking of this family when she'd started it. Instead, like he'd done, she changed the subject. Sitting down again, she had to rack her brain to find something to talk about that had nothing to do with paintings or sex.

"I'm all right now. If you'd like to get back to whoever you came with." He told her who he'd come with. "Well, I'm sure your family misses you."

"I don't think they will right away." He stretched out his legs in front of him and under her chair. It was intimate, the way he was sitting, and when he spoke, she had to have him repeat it. She'd been deep in a fantasy about him being naked in this same position. "I asked if I could kiss you."

She stood so fast that her dress caught under his shoes. Instead of falling, which she was sure she was going to do anyway, it ripped from the top of her shoulder down to the split at the side. Trying to get herself covered, she felt her temper snap.

"What were you doing with your big feet on my dress? Do you have any idea how much this cost?" He didn't answer, but he did stand and push her hands out of the way. "What the fuck are you doing? I can dress myself."

"I'm sure you can, but all you're doing is showing me your lovely nipple, and as much as I'd like to take it in my mouth, I think you'd hit me. Or worse. Just let me tie it." When he had her dress tied at the shoulder again, she kept holding onto the rest. As soon as he told her to turn when he took off his jacket, she put her arms through the sleeves before she could think. "Now, this should hide your pretty parts from anyone while I take you to your hotel. Garrett said he could make excuses for you."

"How do you know?" Lincoln told her that they had a connection, and he spoke through that link to tell him she needed to go home. "Does he know that I tore my dress with your help?"

"If I had told him that, he would have cheered me on in getting my mate naked. I thought that if I just told him you had a headache you'd be able to show your face to him next time." She felt her cheeks heat up then. "Unless, of course, you invite me to spend the night with you. Then he can say whatever he wants."

"You don't want to do that." He was guiding her to the back door and his car before he asked why he'd not. "Because we just met. Even if that wasn't a good excuse, I don't even know if I like you or not. Or if this is going to work."

"Well, let's find out." Grace didn't know what she was going to say, if anything, but he took her mouth and she saw stars. Even on a yucky night like this, they burst behind her eyelids even as the rain fell on her face. Christ, the man sure could kiss. When he lifted his head all she could do was stare at him. "What's your opinion?"

"On what?" He laughed gently, and she had to smile. "Oh, you mean the kiss. It was all right. I mean, you sort of caught me off guard or I would have shown you what a kiss really is."

"Then show me. I'm at your mercy." She started to tell him no, that she wasn't going to subject herself to his kind of treatment, no matter how wonderful it was, but he spoke again. "Or are you afraid that I'm better?"

It was a childish taunt to get her to do what he wanted, and she fell for it. Pulling his head toward hers, his mouth barely above hers, she licked his warm lips before taking the lower one into her mouth and nibbling on it. His moan made her wet; the thong that she had on, she knew, wasn't going to be worth shit by the time she was finished. But when he grinned at her again, she had a feeling that he knew just what was wrong with her and that she was burning up to have him take her.

"I can smell you, the way your body wants me to fill you, to fuck you right here." The words were crude, but the way he said them made her wetter still. "If I were to run my fingers through your lips, touching your hard clit, would you come for me?"

"You're not nice." Lincoln kissed her again, moving between her legs so his cock was at her pussy. Riding him now, not getting any help from him, she cried out when he was suddenly at her breast, his mouth making her nipple hard, her breast swelling with more need. And when he nipped her hard enough to draw blood, she was sure she came loud enough for the entire parking lot to hear. "More. I need more of you."

He sat her on the hood of a car, and when she was reaching for his pants to unbutton them, he tore her panties off. Panting now, she was dizzy with need. And when his cock was free, she wrapped her hand around him and moaned again.

"You're going to make me come all over you if you keep that up." She told him she saw nothing wrong with that. "But then I can't come deep inside of you. Fill that hot pussy of yours until you scream out my name. Will you, Grace? Scream for me when you come, telling the world that I belong to you?"

He moved her hands. They had stilled anyway when he said that he belonged to her. And when he was filling her, his hands lifting her up so she could ride him, all she could think

42

about was this man, his cock, and that he was inside her.

Her body was being pounded, hard enough that the car she was on was rocking. And when he cupped her breast, pulling it up so that he could suckle at it, she threw back her head and gave him whatever he wanted. She was as close to coming as she'd ever been, and he was making her want it all.

"Come for me. Bite me and come."

She wanted to do both. To taste his blood while it went down the back of her throat while he filled her body. When she felt his body stiffen over hers, she moved to his throat and bit down as hard as she could. As soon as his blood filled her mouth, she came with him, screaming around the blood filling her mouth while he took her harder than before.

When she thought him finished, he pulled out and leaned her over the hood of the car. Entering her from this end, he yanked her body to his and she cried out. His hands squeezed her breasts like he was trying to milk them. All the while all she wanted to do was come again, feel him coming inside her like this. And when his fingers slid over her nubbin, Grace screamed again at the release and felt her entire world just snap out and her body go limp.

When she opened her eyes, they were in a car. A limo, she thought, and she started to pull from his embrace. He held her until she struggled more, then she sat across from him on the other seat. She was wearing his jacket and her torn dress, and nothing more.

"What did we just do?" He asked what she meant. "We had sex against a car that wasn't even yours, didn't we? Christ, I'm an idiot. I didn't...I don't suppose you used any kind of protection, did you?"

"You're not carrying my child, Grace. As much as I'd like that, your timing is off. Besides, as a human, you can't have a child of mine. But we can adopt should you want to. I'd be great with that." She wanted to slap the smug look off his face. "You're upset."

"You're damned right I am. I had sex with a stranger." He told her they were no longer strangers. "Oh yes we are. I know nothing about you other than the little bit you told me. And I don't sleep around."

She realized that she was yelling at him when the glass behind her rolled up. The man driving would have heard everything, and that made her more upset. Grace just wanted to go home. Alone. And she wanted to think. Or not think about this anymore.

"You're not staying with me." He said all right, like he wasn't planning on it anyway. "You don't want to?"

"I'm trying to be gentlemanly, but you're snipping and snapping at me like I harmed you somehow." She told him again, this time with clenched teeth, that she didn't sleep around. "I get that. I'm glad you made an exception to that rule for me. But even if you won't admit it, it was the best sex I've ever had. And will ever again."

"I didn't enjoy it at all. You took advantage of me." She knew that wasn't true the moment she said it. "I want you to stay away from me from now on. I mean it."

"All right. But you're not telling me the truth. You enjoyed that as much as I did. In fact, I would say more so." She slapped him then and watched as the mark turned bright pink under the lights of the limo. "Do you feel better?"

He knocked on the glass, and when it rolled down, he

told the driver to pull over and let him out. When the limo stopped, he opened the door and sat there long enough for her to realize that he was as pissed as she was. The problem was, she had no reason to be, and he did.

"Phillip is the driver for our family. He'll take you wherever you want to go, but know that if I ask, he'll tell me where you are. But I won't. You seem to be bent on me not knowing a damned thing about you, even after what we shared." He got out then and the door slammed shut.

Grace sat there while the car started to move again and wondered what she'd just done. Phillip asked where she was staying, and she told him. Then she asked him not to tell Lincoln. His "No, ma'am" sounded like he thought it was funny, but she didn't care. She was confused and hurt. Not at Lincoln, but at herself. What had she just done?

She'd had the best sex of her life with a man she'd only known a few hours. And she knew, as surely as she was sitting here, that no matter how many men took her bed after this, she'd never have it that good again. Grace did something that she'd not done in a very long time. She cried. And while it didn't make her feel any better, she did it until the car stopped in front of her hotel.

~~~

Lincoln went home that night. As soon as Phillip returned he asked if he minded taking him. When he said that he had to take the family to the hotel, then he'd be back, Lincoln told him never mind, that he'd rent a car. He didn't want to put him or the family out because he was pissed off.

Instead of renting a car—everything was closed anyway—he waited until it was nearly midnight and flew home. As always, he was careful of planes and other things going through the air at night. It took him less than an hour, and when he was home he went straight to the wooded area behind his house.

He'd been chopping wood for the fireplace he had put in. It was hard work, but it was also a stress reliever. Right now, he figured that he could easily chop down the forest and it wouldn't be enough. As he started on his next bunch, he was finally calm enough that he could think beyond her blaming him.

There were several things about her that made him mad enough to beat her bottom. But there were many more that had him wanting to find her and talk to her again. She was smart, witty. A little on the mean side, but she'd been confused, and he had added to it, he supposed. Grace was also tantalizing and beautiful. Her talent was beyond what he'd ever expected, and she was humble enough she didn't see what others did. And she had a complexity that he wanted to explore for the rest of his life.

He smelled Tristan before he heard him. There was some sort of sixth sense about the six of them that they could tell which one was coming close to them. He supposed it really was his smell, but Lincoln thought it was something else too. Perhaps the fact that they were all each other had and that made it so they could find them when they needed. Whatever it was, he only just then realized it was daylight and his family was probably wondering what had happened to him.

"So, this is where you come to blow off steam. You've been busy. If it matters to you, Grace isn't talking either. Not that she has to; we kind of know what went on." He looked at

Tristan and told him to fuck off. "You've been busy out here, as I said. Is it sexual frustration or simply frustration? What do you have, ten or twelve cords of wood? Are you planning to burn her body in effigy, or just burn the house down?"

"The woman is nuts." Tristan said nothing but sat on one of the many logs he'd split. "We had this great sex, and then she tells me that I took advantage of her. Then she slapped me."

"What did you say to her?" He said there wasn't any chance to say anything. "I see. Actually, I don't. But you might like to know that she's as confused and upset as you are. Are you going to talk to her?"

"Nope." He split three more logs before stacking them on the cord that he was filling. "I'm done trying to figure out women. And that one is mean. And violent. Did I tell you that she slapped me?"

"Yes, you did. Mean? I don't think I would describe her as that. Upset? Yes, without a doubt. Stressed? Oh yes. But unlike you, she doesn't have an outlet for it. Unless you count you. Then there is that. Do you suppose that she might have been embarrassed about something and took it out on you?" He told his brother that was more than likely what it was. But he wasn't budging. "Then it's your head. Oh yeah, Cooper doesn't think that you forced her into anything, but he's coming to talk to you."

He stacked the rest of the wood up after Tristan left. Lincoln wasn't sure what he had wanted in the first place, but now that he was gone, he realized that he was exhausted. Going to his house to shower and change, he was glad now that no one was up when he came home. While changing his clothing, he ripped the tux to shreds, then sniffed it while taking it out to the trash. It smelled just like she had when she came.

Breakfast was his usual juice and cereal, like the kind a ten-year-old would eat. As old as they all were, they didn't eat as much as other beings. But his breakfast was his time. He would plan out his day and make adjustments as he drove to work, just as he was doing right now. He'd been thinking about the expansions on the greenhouse for a couple days.

When he got there, Cooper was waiting. "Your mate is pissed off." He told him that he wasn't in such a good mood either. "Want to tell me what happened? I don't think it was anything bad, but sometimes talking about it helps."

"No, I do not. But I will tell you that no one is going to force her or me into anything. I'm not going to see her until I'm ready." He asked when that would be. "I don't know, Cooper, when I'm ready is when I'll know. Why?"

"She's leaving." He asked when. "I don't know. And she's convinced Ginger to go with her, that she'd help her with the kids. There's something else you might want to think about. Walton is out. They don't know what happened there, but his father came to see him last night while we were away, and after he left around nine-thirty, Walton wasn't in his cell at midnight. It looked like he'd never been there."

"Inside job?" He said that it looked like it. "Did you send Carson to figure it out? I mean, she'd have the best knowledge about that."

"She went over first thing this morning. And all she could figure out so far was that someone let him out the side door and he rode off with his father. Also, and this will piss you off more, his father saw him in one of the conference rooms rather than the usual cell area. Winnie is helping Carson decide what needs to be done now." Lincoln looked at the marketplace, then his brother again when he continued. "We're losing a great deal more than your mate and our accountant with this, Lincoln. She's going to get herself killed, and that sister of hers too. Ginger won't stand a chance going against a man like Walton. He has a couple screws lose."

"Neither will Grace if it comes to that. Unless it's a verbal contest, and she'll win hands down." He asked if he was going to fix this. "Fix what? She already has me dubbed as the bad guy. And blaming me for us having sex."

"I'm not even going to ask if you forced her. I know better. But what did happen last night, Lincoln? The couple times I saw you, you seemed to be getting along." He told him the highlights of last night. "Sounds like she might have been embarrassed at giving in so easily. And the fact that it was outside."

"That's what I think too, but I can't go and ask her. She doesn't want me to know where she was staying last night." He said that Grace and Ginger were at his house right now. "Packing, I guess."

"No. I mean they probably are, but Carson wanted to see the kids again, and she invited them over for lunch. She had to promise Grace that you weren't there." Lincoln said he was sorry. "I'm not. However, if you were to show up now, looking for me, then you would be just then coming around instead of being there in the first place. Get what I'm saying to you?"

"Yes, I'm not stupid. But she's going to be pissed at you,

I think." He said that he could handle her. "Grace was really angry last night. And as much as I wanted to remain calm, when she told me that I took her, it hurt. I'm sorry, I sound like a child." They were walking toward his car.

"You don't. But you had better fix this. I'm sure that once she leaves, there will be— We need to go. Now." They started running to the cars. "Walton was spotted on the grounds, and Carson wants us to come back. Grace saw him."

Lincoln wanted to fly home, but it was too bright out and he'd scare a great many people trying to get to his mate. As he was turning his truck around, he thought of all the things Walton could do to Grace. And hurting her sister or the kids would be what he'd do to make her pissed off.

It only took them about twenty minutes to get back to Cooper's, but it was long enough for the police to have arrived and search the woods. He asked if the pack was around and was told that four had been killed by Walton. Now, not only were they searching for him, but the pack and police were as well. As soon as Lincoln walked in the door, he looked for Grace. She came to him and threw herself into his arms like she'd done it a million times before. And he found that he liked being her support.

"I'm so sorry. I'm an idiot." He held her, trying to figure out what was going on now. She was sort of high strung, and he didn't want to piss her off again. "I got back to my hotel and realized what a fool I'd been. That I'd lashed out at you because I was so self-conscious and embarrassed. I felt stupid. I'm so sorry."

She looked up at him then, and he wiped the tears away from her cheeks. "Are you all right now? I mean, I don't have to look for a dagger you're going to hit me in the back with?" She smacked him on the chest and started to pull away. "Not yet, please. I've been calling myself all kinds of a fool too for letting you be angry at me. And now I hear we're leaving."

"We're leaving? I didn't realize you were too. Is it because of me?" He said where she went, he was going. "I don't want to leave, but my sister is afraid of.... Well, that he'd get out, and now he has. I don't want them hurt."

"We're dragons, remember? A puny human isn't going to bother us overly much." She laughed. "I have a house we can all live in together. It's huge." She looked at her sister holding Wendall as he cried. "She needs to sit and calm down to nurse him. I was a doctor once in all my lives, and women can't nurse when they're upset. The milk doesn't drop where the baby can get it. Take her to the living room and stay with her. I'll be in when I make some arrangements to have you both brought to my house. All right?" At her consent, he went to find out what he could do to make them safer.

He'd had more security put around the house and barns last night—or earlier this morning when he'd been chopping wood. His brother hadn't been his only visitor. He knew of a couple things in the house that would also keep them safe.

There was a tunnel, of all things, that went from the house to the barn, where there was a fallout shelter. He'd only discovered it by chance when he'd been in the basement looking around. If need be, he'd put the four of them down there until this thing with Walton could be fixed. And by that, he meant for the man to be dead. To Lincoln that was the only way to take care of a mad dog—to put it down for good.

Chapter 4

Grace couldn't have been more in love with the house than if he'd read her mind and created what she'd always dreamed of in one. The big balcony off the master bedroom where she was had her wanting to bring her bed out there and sleep. Then there were the large his and hers closets that just screamed for her to fill them. She wouldn't, of course, but it was nice to have all the room.

"I've not done much in here but put in a bed." She turned and looked at him. "Do what you want in here, I don't care. So long as I can sleep with you, it could be bright pink for all I care. I'd prefer earth tones, but I can live with whatever you want."

"It won't be pink. I can't handle that color, much less a bedroom. I love the earth tones as well, like the ones in the living room. I'd like to stick with that." He nodded and handed her a thick envelope. "What's this?"

"The deed to the house. It's been put in your name. And

before you say anything, we needed to do that because we don't die. The next time we need to resume our lives, it'll be in my name and so on until we adopt children. Then they'll take a turn at it." She asked why he'd say that to her, talking about dying so soon after meeting. "I'm sorry, but you won't die either, love. The moment we touched, you became what I am. As your sister is as well. I believe she touched the wings of a faerie, and that was her gift for not harming them."

"I'm an immortal? As in, I'm not going to die?" He nodded. But before she could ask what exactly that meant, he moved to the bathroom that was as big as her living room at her old house. "What does that mean? There's something wrong with that statement. How will I ever die?"

"You can from being beheaded. But if anyone gets that close to you, they'll be burnt toast. And then there is blood poisoning. Though now that I think on it, I'm not sure iron would harm you. But then there is the shot to the heart. That one will be harder to do since I'm never leaving your side when we're out." He stretched, and she wanted him right then. But she had to focus on what he was saying. "Also, you'll have to have a faerie. All dragons do—we're very closely bonded together. Mine is Drizzle. I'm not sure why he likes to be called that, but that's what he told me. He's usually off running things for me when I'm home. Otherwise he's right there with me. Same as you— I'm overwhelming you, aren't I?"

"Yes, and not a little bit either. Why do I need a faerie? I'm assuming it's because of safety concerns. I'm not really keen on having someone with me all the time." While she was talking, he moved for her to see the railing, and there stood about half a dozen of the cutest little people she'd ever seen. Walking toward them, she asked if these were all hers, but spoke to them before she got an answer. "I love that you came here to see me even if you're not going to be with me. My goodness, you're wonderfully shiny too."

She wondered if she had insulted them when their wings fluttered quickly. But when they bowed, she curtsied for them. It was a thing that just popped into her head. Something that she'd not done as a child, yet it seemed appropriate. They smiled at her and she returned it.

"Mistress? Lady Manning, my name is Rose. I am the faerie for the king." Grace had forgotten Cooper was the king of dragons. "This is, in order of where they are, Piney, Jackson, Benson, and Tulip. They have come to see which of them would serve you."

"I guess I'm just too new at this; serve me how?" They explained what would go on and how they were to help her. "That sounds so wonderful. To have someone do small things for me would be nice, I think. I'm not so sure how much I could use someone all the time. I'm used to doing things for myself. But if I must have a faerie, how do I pick one of you, and what happens to the others?"

"They will go back to the flower fields. It is their job, you see." She did, but didn't want to pick only one. She really did want all four to be with her, just to keep them out of the fields. That sounded like a hard job, and if she could, she wanted to save them from that. "If you wish, my lady, they can all work with you. But it will be most difficult on you and them if they don't have enough to do. Boredom is bad for a faerie."

"We get into trouble a great deal when we're not working."

Jackson smiled, then blushed when he spoke. She could see that. Their wings were moving miles a second, and she would bet it was nervous energy. "Piney and I, we're from the same picking. Benson is the oldest, and Tulip the youngest. You can take any of us, mistress, and it'll be all right. There are more brides coming, and perhaps they'll pick one of the others." A decision came to her while they were standing there. But she asked what they meant by a picking.

"The queen of all faeries comes to the flowers where we are born and picks us up to make our wings work." Tulip smiled at her as she continued. "Sometimes, when we're not picked up, we can become big, like a human, and help them in ways they do not know. I have a sister that works in the human world, and she loves it. She likes people."

With her decision made, she looked at Rose, then Lincoln. She had a feeling that he knew what she was going to do but said nothing to him. He had a big enough head as it was. So, she turned her attention to Rose.

"I want all four. I could use two with me during the times I'm not painting, and the other two for when I'm working. They can trade off if they wish. But the ones in the work area, they'll have to learn to clean brushes for me, pick up lids when I drop them. Things like that. Okay?" She was getting the best of the best, she thought when they all nodded. "I'm a very messy painter too. But I love it quiet when I'm working. Not even any music. You'll have to remember that, please?"

"Then you should take Benson with you there. He is very quiet and he's a hard worker. He can't sing either." The man bowed before her, and she looked at Lincoln when he laughed. "Sir?"

"You are going to love having them around all the time. And I'm betting it won't matter how much you keep them busy, you'll be getting them into trouble too." She smacked him again. "All right, I'll tell you how to care for them because they would never presume to ask for anything they need. It can be annoying when you forget something, but we'll work together on that. They need to have fresh flowers when we can get them, and water. I usually leave some on each of the floors for Drizzle."

"I'm going to write this down." Benson followed her into the bathroom where she had put her notebook about things that she thought the house could use and what she wanted to bring here from her storage unit. But before she left the room, she saw the older faerie had followed her. "Hello, Benson. Are you ready to work for me?"

"Yes, mistress, it'll be my honor. I just need to ask are you famous? I've had a dream to work for someone famous." She said that she wasn't, and the look of disappointment on his face was priceless. "I might be someday. I sold all my work at the gallery last night."

He perked up and asked where she was going to be working. Actually, she'd not thought of that and told him so. She'd have to ask Lincoln about the big barn, or perhaps the basement. She'd be thrilled to death either way. The house and the people in it were wonderful.

Grace even began to feel better. She didn't feel so angry all the time since coming here. Of course, she was getting laid on a regular basis — at least twice a day, so perhaps more than regularly, but she was most assuredly more relaxed.

She and Lincoln walked out to the two places he said she

could have as a studio with all the faeries. Benson sat on her shoulder and told her things she wouldn't have otherwise noticed. The tree faeries were working on the leaves, he said, getting them ready for fall. There were also brownies about. They were the workhorses, he told her, always making it so the big limbs fell from the trees so as not to harm anything below them. He said that they would fly to the earth to warn others to move when it was about to go. Or sometimes, and this was less dangerous, they'd push the wood from the trees ahead of where they might be working. It was how the other creatures of the earth found homes for themselves, as well as food.

The metal barn was huge, and she figured Lincoln would want to do something with it instead of her taking up the room. But he assured her that he had no use for the place and would be honored if she took it. Honored? Well, she would take him up on the deal. To have so much space without anyone bothering her would be just what she needed. Especially since talking to Garrett and him already asking for more work.

"What do you do? I mean, other than be very rich?" Lincoln laughed and told her that he saw to businesses. "I have no idea what that means. Do you just buy them then break them apart? Do you put old ladies and children out to the street? Or are you the type of rich person that donates tons of money to half assed causes that don't need it, because the CEO makes more than most people?" She looked at him.

"I can't tell if you're pissed or not. But you keep bringing up my being rich. You are too. I don't know if I've told you or not, but as of the moment you moved in with me, you were my other half. As in, everything, and I do mean everything, I have is now yours. Not half, not a part, but whatever is mine is now yours as well." She asked why he'd do that. "Because I never want you to have to worry about a thing again. Not money, nor whether you can afford anything. If you want to donate all our funds to something, there will always be more. I'm good at making money. Then there is the fact that you're going to be selling enough that I'd never have to work again."

"You mean if I were to go to the bank and tell them to give all the money in the account to the person behind me, you'd say that was all right." He nodded. "No one is that generous."

"Your temper is showing again." Grace tried to bring herself back to her good mood, but she was upset that he'd say something like that and not mean it. "We have more than you could spend in several lifetimes, love. The money in the bank here is only a drop of what we have. I have a castle that has been renovated and brought up to date that we can visit any time you wish. And you'll be happy to know that it, too, is in your name. Being around as long as we have, we were able to amass fortune after fortune and not have to spend a great deal of it. We saved everything we could for a rainy day."

"You're serious." He nodded at her. "How could you be so free with your money? And to put my name, a lowly human, on all your things. I mean, is it true about dragons? Can you really make diamonds from tears?"

She didn't have any idea why she was so angry, but he seemed to not care. Once they were near the building, he sent the faeries inside and stood there looking at her. When she turned away, embarrassed at how she had spoken to him, he brought her face back around and kissed her on the mouth

59

quickly before speaking.

"Lowly human? I would never think of you as lowly anything. You are the bright shining star in my life. The person that makes me a stronger and better dragon. I couldn't care less if you were a wolf, or cat. You are the person that is for me, and I am thrilled beyond words to get to be a part of your life." She wasn't sure what to do with such words. And she knew this time they were sincere. As she lay her head on his shoulder, he continued. "When we were born, we were dragons. Not shifters, but real dragons. My father noticed, unlike a lot of them then, that our population was being murdered. Our bodies were cut up and sold off. And what they couldn't sell, they left to rot in the sun. My own mother had been killed and stripped of everything for greed. So, my father had gone to a great witch and asked for a spell to give us, his six sons, a chance to survive. It was that night, my uncle, Dad's brother, said that he could no longer be in this world. His own family, his children and mate, had been killed not a month before, butchered like they were nothing more than cattle grazing in the fields. His youngest was younger than me at the time. He left us all his gems—his worth, we call it."

"He killed himself?" Lincoln told her that being without his other half, he didn't want to live. And without his children, he felt he had no need of life. "I'm so sorry. I can't imagine the grief that he must have felt. Or the love your father did."

"He did love us. And in doing so, he too died to give us the ability to shift into humans. To walk among them like them so that they'd never know we were what they sought. It was the only way to save us, and it worked. We're the only

60

ones of our kind. Dragons that can shift into humans, rather than the other way. But because of this, we cannot change our mates into what we are. Nor can you have our children, because you cannot bear an egg, which is how we are made. Your body isn't equipped for such a thing. We are also sought after. There are people that would come and take what we have because of a book we own."

"Your life sounds much harder than I thought it would be." Grace looked around, seeing things that she never had before. The faeries of the forest, the other creatures that were there working as if they did this all the time. And she supposed that they did. Without humans knowing it. "I'm sometimes a terrible person. I was just thinking that I was in a better mood all the time, profoundly more relaxed, but then you talk about money and I go off again. Why do I do that?"

"Perhaps you cannot imagine a time when you would no longer worry about things such as money, or where your next meal might be coming from. Or that you have always worried about them and can't fathom not doing so now. I don't know. But I love you, Grace." She looked at him. "I do. I have since the moment you touched me. The second that I figured out that you were for me and me for you. I need to be honest, I never thought that I could be this happy with a mate, but I love you. More than I thought possible. And I wanted you to know that."

"I don't know what I feel about you. You make me feel wonderful. I feel like I can take on the world with you here. I even feel good about myself, which isn't always the case." He said that he could understand that. "Do you? I don't understand how you can be so nice to me when I've mostly been a bitch."

He laughed and took her into the barn. As soon as she entered, Grace wanted to cry. It was no longer just a barn, but her studio. He'd brought all her stuff here and had them set up. There were also items she'd only dreamed of. Things that as a struggling artist, or even just at life, she'd never thought of having.

"This is too much." He said never. The canvas stretcher was begging to be touched, it seemed, and she ran her fingers over the canvas on the roll. "I've always wanted this. I've had to wait until these sorts of supplies went on sale before I could buy them. But never did I dream of having something so nice as this. You've made it so I don't have to worry about that, haven't you?"

"I told you. You're my other half, and I want you to be as happy as I am. Even if you do show me you still have a temper once in a while." She laughed with him but was embarrassed. He had taken the time to get these things for her, and she'd been a mean bitch again. "What are you thinking?"

"How am I ever going to get used to you being nice? I've been nothing but hot and cold since I met you. How the hell are you able to be so nice to me when I'm rarely nice to you?" He kissed her then, and she looked up at him. "You keep this up, Lincoln, and you just might make me fall in love with you despite the type of person I am."

"That's the plan, my love. That's all it has ever been. Not to buy your love, but to make you see that I care enough about you to be your whipping post if you need me. Or your sexual slave if that's what you want."

She was still laughing as they moved around the room.

This was going to be her biggest leap into becoming a real artist, she thought. No more excuses that she couldn't afford something. And Garrett was going to be very happy too. Her muse was already ready to get to work on something new. And Grace was glad to be needed.

~~~

Walton watched his father talk to the police from his hiding place in the kitchen. They'd been by twice now to see if he'd heard from him. Walton thought they were doing a half assed sort of job in locating him, but he didn't care. So long as they left him alone and didn't try to arrest him again. But now that he was out, he was going to take care of his wife and that daughter of hers, and make sure his father never touched his little boy.

He had a son that he was going to raise to be just like him. Well, perhaps not just like him. Walton was going to make sure that his son didn't fear him as he did his own father. Not that he really feared him, but he didn't like him all that much. Mostly it was because he lorded things over him all the time.

Like how he had a record. So, what? Most of the people in this stupid world did and got along fine. Or how he'd never finished college so he didn't have a degree in anything but partying. Again, so what? He could read and write and get by when he needed to. When there was something put before him, he could make out what it was about without having to resort to someone explaining it to him word for word. That was another thing his father did. Over explain things. Like he was some big dummy who wasn't smart enough to get out of the rain. Walton was far from that.

When the police left he went to talk to his father. The fact that he'd lied for him twice now was a good sign. And if he could, he was going to milk that. Now if he could get him to search for his wife, and then give him money, things would start to look up. Walton had plans, and his father, he knew, was going to be standing in the way.

"You didn't tell me that you weren't married to the twat. Why the hell are you even bothering with her if you don't even know for sure if that boy is your son?" He said that he was. "How do you know? You have some sort of crystal ball that tells you these things? Who do you think had sex with her when you weren't home?"

"Because I tied her to the bed when I wasn't fucking her, or to the kitchen table when she was supposed to be working. I had plans, Father. I also had a dragon that was going to make me richer than you are. Because, as you're so fond of telling me, it's not my money but yours, and you're taking it with you." He said that he was. "Well, how do you expect me to make it in this world the way I want with no one to carry on my name? How many times have you said that over the years? And told me that was the only reason you had me."

"Yes, because it's such a stellar name now, thanks to you, isn't it? I made myself into something, Walton. I didn't pander to the needs of my body but went out into the world and made myself a good man. With funds enough that I never had to worry about my son, or who he might have been fathered by." There was so much he could say to that statement, but he didn't. Just looking over at his mother—a milksop, his grandda used to call her—he knew that his father had done no less to his own wife. "I'm a man's man, and you have ruined my good name. I can only hope that that boy of yours is a better person than you. And if I can, I'm going to raise him to be just like me. A man to be proud of."

"What do you mean, you're going to raise him? He's my son, not yours, and you can't have him." He laughed when his father said yes, he would. "You mean the man that taught me that it's okay to beat his wife? I enjoy a good beat down too, by the way. And that if you want it and they tell you no, then take it anyway. You said the golden rule is for suckers, and if I wanted to make it in this world, then I had to be in your image. I found out that wasn't what I wanted. I decided to make myself into who I wanted. Walton Conrad, a great man."

"I taught you the real meaning of being what it would take to make it in this world." His father rubbed his chest again, like he was reaching for a gun or something. "Walton, aren't you the least bit ashamed of how you act? How, even now at twenty-seven, you still don't have a clue what you want to do in this world? By the time I was your age, I had it all planned out. Money that I could turn into something more. You have nothing that I haven't given you."

"I'm thirty-one. Thanks for keeping up on that. And I have plenty that you've not given me." His father looked at his mother when she sighed heavily. "What do you think is going to happen to her when you finally kick the bucket? You think she's going to do the same things? Come down to breakfast at precisely six fifty-one. Go to the women's club at seven twenty-three. Then what? Do you suppose she's any more animated than she is here? I don't think so. You've killed her spirit the same as you have everyone that lives here. Is that what you plan to do if you get my son?"

"Their spirit? What are you talking about? That's for the dead, not someone living in my house. And your mother has finally reached a point in our relationship that she's better off just doing as I tell her, and not making a big deal out of every little thing. Just as you should have learned, but never did." His mother stood and pushed her chair into the table. She looked at him then moved to leave the room, but Father spoke first. "Where are you going? It's not time for you to—"

Had Walton not been sitting there, he would have missed the entire thing. It was over in seconds, both bleeding out when his mother took the steak knife from her service set and brought it from ear to ear across his father's throat. The way his father jerked around, screaming as blood spurted out of his neck, Walton nearly didn't see his mother sliding the same sharp knife across her own throat and then dropping to the floor. Walton was so stunned that he didn't move. He wasn't even sure that he could. Walton had just seen his milksop mother kill his father and then herself. Like she'd been planning this forever.

When someone started to scream, he stood. The cook had been bringing in his coffee and had seen them both dead or dying on the floor. Walton went to look at his mother, to make sure, he supposed, that she was gone. Looking at his dead father, there was no doubt that he had bled out. And his dear mother, who was no longer moving, was staring right up at him with the strangest smile on her face. She had killed him then herself in a matter of seconds.

Moving toward the door that led to the kitchen, he told someone to call the police. Walton knew that he'd not have much time. Grabbing his father's fat wallet from his bloodied jacket pocket, he made his way to the upper floors before the police arrived. He had no idea if the staff would remember to not tell them that he'd been around, so he was making himself scarce. But he was going to get out of there in style, and with all the cash and other items that he could carry.

Raiding his father's room, he found more cash as well as his stash of jewelry. Father never put things in places like a box — no, he had to have them laying out, for anyone to see. And he thought to tempt the staff into stealing from him so that he could teach them a lesson. One that usually put them in the hospital or dead from the beatings. He knew all too well how bad his father treated people who took from him. Had he servants where he lived, he might well have treated them the same. He liked things just so, and they rarely did anything properly as far as he was concerned.

Gathering some clean clothes and stuffing them into a duffel, he slipped out the window on the second floor and escaped down the trellis that led to the backyard. Something that he'd done a thousand times while living here. By the time the police were pulling in front of the house, not only was he nearly to the city limits, but he'd managed to take a car that had been his father's favorite. It wasn't like he was going to use it again, he thought. Driving was much faster than walking anyway, and his father would surely want him to have the best now that he was gone.

His father was dead. The fat fuck was finally dead. And by his own lovely wife's hand. Mother had been a zombie for a very long time, so Walton did wonder what the hell had happened to make her take action today. And now she was dead as well. But to be honest, he thought that she'd been in that condition for quite some time anyway. Or so he would have thought up until she sliced his dad's throat like a Christmas ham.

As he drove to the hotel on the other side of town, he thought of all the things he was going to have to take care of now that his parents were out of his life. Walton did wonder if he would have to make arrangements for his parents but dismissed that right away. His father would never have trusted him with such a task and had more than likely taken care of that himself. It would have been paid for, as would the moaners that were to show up. His father was a detail man all the way to the end.

He more than likely had thought that he'd die long after Mother and had all her holdings left to him. And she'd been the one with the cash when they married. Father just managed to make it into more. Since he was dead first, then Mother, Walton wondered how that would work. Because as far as he could see, he was the sole survivor of the Conrad fortune. Laughing, he thought about what his father would think of that.

"Probably rolling in his own blood about now."

Settling into the hotel room after checking in, Walton turned on the television. He wanted to hear what was being said about the deaths, and if anyone had let it slip that he'd been there too. Walton kept thinking about how quickly his mother had acted. Like she'd been planning this for a very long time and finally got the nerve to do something. He was more like her than he'd thought in that moment. That was just the way he handled things too. Quickly and to the point. Then never look back.

Breaking news came on to talk about the tragedy when he'd been at the hotel for an hour. It said that there was an incident at the Conrad estate, and they were still awaiting word on what had happened. So far, the news reporter had shit and he thought it was funny. If they were to interview him, he could give them a firsthand account of what went down.

At around six that night, after all day of them making speculations about what might have been done to whom, they finally said that Mr. and Mrs. Walter Conrad were both dead by an apparent murder-suicide. There wasn't a note that they could find, but the staff said that they'd been having breakfast as they usually did, and when they came in to serve them, they found Mrs. Conrad on the floor bleeding to death. Mr. Conrad was slumped over in his usual chair, covered in blood. They didn't know what had happened, but they were shocked to find them that way.

"No shit. She just up and killed him, that's what she did. Probably been planning it forever too."

He laughed when the news reporter said that her heart went out to the rest of the family. Like he even cared that his parents were both gone. It just made things easier now that he didn't have to be nickel and dimed every time he wanted a buck or two. He was richer than he'd ever dreamed he'd be. Nothing would have to be shared with any other family member, and he was glad. He might have had to take his own steak knife to someone if that were the case.

He'd have money enough to get the equipment he needed to not just get the kid back who the dragon had befriended, but also the means to hold the dragon once he got it. And by

God, he would too. Just as soon as he found his fucking wife. Then he was going to kill her, take his son and all his riches, and live like the king he'd always wanted to be.

Walton wished now that he'd have killed Ginger when he had the chance. That bitch from the mountain had fucked that all up for him. Some butch dike he was going to kill too. Maybe. He would only admit this to himself, but she scared him a bit. The way she held him there with nothing but her hands. But he'd deal with her when and if he had to. For now, he was focusing on Ginger and that daughter of hers. She was going to get him that dragon, or he'd kill her. He was going to anyway, but she was useful to him now, and he would be just as happy to use and abuse her like he did her mother.

"Yes, sir, I'm going to be on rich street soon." He laughed when he saw the woman talking again and didn't even bother turning the sound back up. She'd told him all he needed to know, they were both dead and he wasn't blamed for it. "Life is good for a change. Yes, sir, life is what you make it, and thanks to dear Mother, mine is sitting pretty damned good for a change."

Chapter 5

Sadie sat on the rocker and waited for the household to wake. She wasn't in any hurry—not that she didn't have things to do, but she knew they'd be there when she went back. Watching over the Manning boys had been something she'd promised their father she'd do. But now it was time to give them the rest of the spell. She had been waiting for the right moment, and it had finally come.

Rose came to sit with her just as she was closing her eyes. She wasn't one to put your guard down around. She took her job very seriously when it came to her king. It had been a good choice to have the then young faerie pair with the king of dragons.

"He thinks you've come to harm them." She asked Rose if she'd told him why she was here. "Nay, I did not. 'Tis not my job. You have come to finish this, haven't you? It's about time, if you ask me."

"I did not, but you are correct. I should have arrived

before the first mate did, and now there are three of them." Rose sat down on her leg, not bothering with the formality between them. "He is well, the king of all dragons?"

"He is the best, my lady. His mate, she is so much more than we would ever have thought for one such as him. I worried at first that he was making a mistake, but she turned out to be his lead in a lot of their ventures. It is good to see him so happy." Sadie nodded and said that was as it should be. "Do you know what the magic you bring has for them?"

"No, I was told only to wait until the time was right. I had no idea what that would mean when I gave their sire the magic. Just when I was about to find them, they found me. I think that is the perfect timing, do you not?" Rose said that she didn't know about any of this. "You know more than you allow people to see. You always have."

"I am but a faerie." Sadie snorted and they both laughed. "He will know soon enough what it is I have done for him. Do you think he'll be upset with me? And for not telling him of the other work I do for him and his brothers?"

"I doubt that he'd ever be mad at you for very long. And you've no reason to tell him everything, only what you wish to. But I think him not to care if he is anything like his father." Rose moved to stand on her hand and Sadie brought it to her face to better look at her. "You have grown into a beauty, my little Rose."

"Thank you, my lady. Coming from you, that means a great deal." She sat down on her outstretched palm. "Do the slayers yet come? Should we be more careful now that a child is on the way?"

"They are all but gone. That doesn't mean they won't rise

again though. Like a wart, you can never get the root for all the tangles in the skin." Rose nodded. "You and your kind, you are well taken care of? You have enough of the gardens to keep you warm and fed?"

"We've more than enough. And Lincoln has opened a greenhouse, and given us permission to take what we wish from it, so long as we want. He too is a good man, and a leader among humans. They do not know the strength of him, but I do." She asked if she'd talked to him about the things she wanted him to do. "Not yet. I've been awaiting word from you. Besides, his mind is befuddled, what with him having a new mate and a business."

Sadie laughed; oh, how she remembered those times. But her mate had been gone for longer than they were together. At times she would forget that she'd even had one, it had been so very long. That didn't mean that she didn't still miss him.

"His lordship has arisen. He will be down soon. Will you wait here to talk to him, or go inside? It will be better if you could talk to them both at one time. He will be more inclined to hold his tongue until you are finished than not, with Lady Carson there." She said that she'd go inside if it was all right. "Yes. I will have cook, Mistress Molly, make you some tea. It will help your old bones."

"You talk to me about that when I know you are older than me." Rose landed on her shoulder and guided her to the big kitchen. Sitting, she laid her burden and cane to the side. "I should like something sweet too, not too terribly so, please."

Molly fussed around for her, and she ended up with two scones as well as a cup of coffee, not tea. It was more to her liking than tea. She knew that the dragons didn't partake in the stuff, but she had found that it did her little harm, and she loved the rich nutty taste of it. This cup was very good, and she sipped it gently.

The big man that entered the kitchen looked so much like his father that she nearly spit out her brew. "My goodness, how you have grown. And into such a man too. I had no idea that you could be so handsome." He was upset, she could tell that, but didn't let it bother her. He would accept what she had for him or not, it mattered very little to her. "Your mother and father have been moved to this estate. I have had the faeries get permission from the queen to—"

"I was going to do that." Sadie told him she was sorry, but she wished for him to be happy. "To make me so, you would need tell me why you are here so early in the morning, and why you've come in the first place."

"Your father has sent me." He told her that he was dead. "I know that well enough. I gave him the magic that took his life to make it so that his sons would have theirs. You have done well with his sacrifice over the years. He'd be very proud of you."

"We have worked hard to make it so that he would have been." She nodded and asked after his family, hoping that his mood would improve with the question. "They are all well, as you know. You have been spying on us these last years, haven't you?"

"Cooper, what a way to talk to someone." This must be the lovely mate. And what a beauty she was. Sadie wanted to bow but knew that she'd never get back up if she did. "You must be the famed Sadie they're all abuzz about. I'm Carson Manning. I will tell you now, if you harm any of my family, you're dead where you stand."

"Yes, my lady." She would too. There was no doubt in her mind whatsoever. "I've come to give you the last of the magic, and things that your father wanted you to have."

"I don't think I want it." She asked Cooper why not. "I don't know. It might be from anyone and you're trying to kill me."

"What a thing to say." She laughed, then stood and opened the leather bag that she'd held in trust all these years. After dumping it on the table, she stared at the young man and smiled. "Your father was my friend, and he was a good man who loved you all very much. He told me that someday you'd be ready for this, and that I was to bring it to you. However, I was too late. No, not that, but a little late. I was to come before the mates did. This is from him, written in my hand because, as you know, your father could neither read nor write." She started for the door but was stopped by Carson. "I must go. I have brews still on the fires. I only came here to give him this."

"Wait." She looked at Cooper as he stood there with a large key in his hand. She knew it was going to give them memories. "Where is the trunk for this? And what is this book about?"

"The trunk is in my lair. If you don't trust me, and it is apparent that you don't, then I shall have it brought here for you. Otherwise, you may come at any time and open it. On second thought, I'll have it brought here. It has some pictures and such in it that he thought you'd enjoy." She looked at the book. "You have a book of the dragons, don't you? Well, this is the second. There is one more, and I don't have any idea where it is. If it even exists any longer. But you may want to read the first couple pages. Your father was a good and gifted man."

She'd done all that she could concerning the package and started for the door. Sadie was in the yard when two faeries came to be with her. Both Daniel and his mate, Petunia, were her friends, and if anyone could cheer her after the treatment from their king, then they could.

Sadie had been living in the cave since she woke from her rest for nearly ten decades now. It was a place that she could both see the young men growing up as well as do what she needed to keep them safe. And she had, a great deal over the years. But only recently was it apparent that they no longer needed her. And since then, she had been feeling all her years, as well as losing her ability to stand for long periods of time. Just as she was ready to take a little rest before going up the mountain, she sat down on the ground and thought about the distrust from Cooper.

"He has been dealt a great deal in the last months." She told Daniel that she understood his attitude. "His father would beat him should he have heard him talking to you thusly. He was not kind to you."

"And who can blame him? He is a man trying to make his way in the world, even after all this time. Nay, I don't blame him at all. Mistrust, whoever it is placed on, it is a good thing when trying to keep all those that you love from being harmed." Petunia sat beside her and she put out her hand of flowers that she'd picked. The faerie took one and started to nibble on it while she continued. "What would you have done if he had welcomed me with open arms? He still believes that I am the one that killed their beloved father. It's normal. Especially for Cooper. He, until recently, hated all humans and what they brought him. It only stands to reason that he would be leery of me."

"He should not be, that is all I'm saying." Standing, she started for the hill again when she felt the earth speaking to her. Waiting till she understood the lady of the earth, she moved to go back to the house. "Run ahead for me, Daniel, and tell his lordship that he needs to come to me now. There is trouble brewing."

He flew to the house, and she feared that he'd not return with the man. Not only did he come out of the house and toward her, but his queen did as well. As soon as he was near her, he scooped her into his arms and took her to the house. Such muscles the man had, and today she was grateful for them.

"I've heard from the earth." He told her to hush, that he needed to make sure she was all right. "I'm old, Lord Cooper, very old, and need to speak with you."

"Why are women so stubborn? I will get you some juice, then you can talk." She told him she could speak while it was being brought to her. "All right then, tell me what you heard."

"There is a man coming—his name is Walton. He wants the child so she can tame the dragons." Cooper asked if he was taming them or that she could lure them. "I can't tell. He only thinks of it that way. The child is friends with one. I cannot see his name."

"Waco. But she didn't train him. She befriended him, and he her. In fact, he protected her." Sadie said that was him. The earth had only said that he was her protector. "This man, he

77

tried to kill her when she was trying to get away from him. Her mother and unborn child as well. Ginger has since given birth, but the little boy was shot in the process."

"Yes, yes, but he comes here. You mustn't let him have her." He said that he wouldn't. "But he'll use whatever means necessary to take her from her home. You must keep him from harming her." Carson asked why it was so important; not that they'd not keep her safe, but why this child. "Because she really can train them."

~~~

Lincoln watched Grace as she painted on the canvas. It was erotic the way she moved back and forth, how she chewed on the end of her brush as she looked at her progress. He even thought the way she stood was sexy. He had it bad for his mate, and he found that he didn't really care who knew it.

"Will you stop looking at me like I'm a side of beef?" He laughed when she did, but she put her work down. "Don't you have something to do that isn't in here? I have to get at least six paintings done in a month, and you're distracting me."

"I could go, but I don't really want to." She told him to make himself want to. "All right, but I hate it. I love watching you work."

"I never thought I'd say this to you, but I don't want to see you again until supper. Go away. I really do need to work." He kissed her on the mouth but only a small peck because she pulled back and threatened him with a wet paint brush. "I mean it—don't return until I need you or call you to supper."

He left. Lincoln didn't want to, but he knew that, just like him, she had things to do. Instead of going in the house, as that was where he was headed, he decided to find one of his brothers and see if they'd keep him from being bored. The greenhouse project no longer needed him to be there.

Lincoln had hired Ginger. There wasn't a doubt that he would, he supposed, but she had taken all the worry out of his job and made it easier for him. Not only that, but she had come up with a map of the entire project and where there were empty spaces, as well as who was now paying a yearly rent as opposed to month to month. Then after talking it over with Cooper, he hired her to manage the entire project and walked away. Not nearly as difficult as he'd thought it would be. Now he needed to find something else to do.

What are you doing right now? Xavier told him he was playing a game of chess with Foster. *I need something to do. I don't suppose you have a project that might need help, do you?*

You could paint walls at the building on Tenth. I did such a poor job of it that they sent me home in shame. Which I suppose is good. I didn't care for it anyway. He didn't think he'd like it any better and told him that. *You should contact Lucas — he's got several things going on right now, and you could get on his nerves like you did Grace's.*

She told you? Xavier said that he'd asked where he was, and she'd told him she'd kicked him out. *I was bothering her by thinking of all kinds of ways I could take her against her new equipment. Yesterday we got a pug mill. It has nothing to do with dogs, believe it or not. As well as the makings of a raku kiln. Grace told me that she loves to work in clay to get inspiration. I have no idea. Anyway, I'll contact Lucas.*

Instead of reaching out, he simply walked to his house. It wasn't that far, and he needed to burn off some energy. He'd think that as much sex as he was having, he'd be exhausted all the time. But the opposite was true. He was much more energized than ever before.

His brother was on the phone when he was let in the house. There was as much going on inside as there was in Grace's work area. When Lucas finally hung up, he growled loudly then sat down hard in his chair.

"You ever have one of those days when not a damned thing goes your way?" Lincoln told him all the time. "Today is one of those for me. Alan is on vacation."

"Oh Christ." He nodded. Lincoln wanted to laugh, but in his current mood, Lucas might hurt him. "I came to see if I could help, but I can't do Alan's job. No one can. I can't believe you allowed him to go."

"I know. But he deserved it. And I do have to let him occasionally. I think I'll make it more enticing next year. If he stays, I'll double his check for the two weeks." He asked if he was going to be gone that long, thinking of all the shit the man did for Lucas. "No, thank goodness. Just one. And I promised myself I'd not bother him unless his new computer was on fire."

"How many times have you called him?" Lucas only grinned. "That bad, huh? Has he threatened to quit yet? If not, I'm sure you can at least call once or twice more."

"I knew he did a lot for me, but I am at a total loss here. I don't know the filing system as well as he does. And I came up with the way to do it. I haven't any idea how to get into my calendar. And I've been tempted to send him my appointments and have him put them in from there. But he did tell me the last time I called, if I did again, then he would erase all my contacts and I'd have to start over. No quitting yet, but he is threatening me."

Lincoln laughed. "Tell me what you need and let me see if I can get things going for you. I know enough about computers that I don't mess up too badly." Lucas was shaking his head. "What is that for? I need something to do."

"Not with the system, thank you very much. He really would quit if I did anything wrong to it." Lucas leaned back in his chair. "He did do some things for me before he left. I am a sort of free man for the whole week. Alan didn't make any appointments, so I could work on the sixteen proposals that have been on my desk for two weeks."

"Now that is something I do." He handed him half. "I meant help, not do them all."

"I have to get these done, seriously. There are four businesses right now that could use our help. And if you could research some for me, it'll make it easier to come to a decision." He nodded and looked at the first name. "Thanks, Lincoln. And just so you know, Grace said I was to make you stay here for at least four hours."

"What did she do, contact you all?" Lucas said pretty much. "I'll have to make her pay. I can think of hundreds of ways to have her make it up to me."

"Yeah, well, for now, research."

He worked on the first for ten minutes before he heard the phone ring again. Lucas said he'd turn the service on after it hung up. As he dug deeper into the man who wanted a loan to keep his building afloat, the more intrigued he became about the man's lies.

"This guy is so full of shit. I'd be tempted to loan him the money just to see how he squirms his way out of paying us back. He's very creative with his needs." Lucas asked how. "He said that he has a sick mother and that she's drained his accounts. But on page two, he tells how she had died several years ago and that her illness wiped him out. Then on page four of his letter to you, he tells how his mother is in fine health, and was willing to help him without pay until he gets back on his feet."

"You can put that in the hell no pile. I had one I was looking at yesterday that said right out since we had all the money in the world, he didn't feel the need to have arrangements to pay us back. He said that he thought it would be nice to have a long vacation once in a while, and that we should want him to. Happy employees, he said, make a happy boss." Lucas stood and got them both a bottle of water. "People amaze me at times. Where do they come up with these things? I can see them lying in bed, thinking of ways to not borrow, but not to take the money and run away with it. I filed it with the other one."

They both worked for two hours. It was actually sort of fun. They talked over the proposals for several of the buildings downtown, as well as the storefronts asking for help to get their business up to code or simply looking better. All in all, they turned down all but one asking for a loan, and three for improvement money.

"Thank you. Christ, I need to just look them over when they come in instead of piling them up until they're overwhelming. I say that, but we both know in a few weeks, I'm going to have another stack needing the same information." Lincoln told him it was his pleasure. "How about some lunch? My treat since you kept me on target today. I might even make some brownie points with Alan when he gets back. In four days, sixteen hours, and twenty-three minutes. Give or take a few minutes."

There weren't a lot of places to just have a fast lunch in town. One of the many proposals—this one they kept in the keeper pile—was to put in a little place that would serve sandwiches and soup during lunchtime hours. Lincoln thought that he could get behind something like that. It was his favorite kind of lunch treat.

"The woman that wanted to put in a yarn shop, did you know that she is the same person that wanted to put in a fabric store several years ago?" Lucas said that he didn't. "I think there might be something going on there. Nothing nefarious or anything like that, but I know for a fact that she makes quilts for extra money, as well as knitting. Perhaps she's hoping to have a store so that she can buy her product at wholesale."

"You think that's all it is?" Lincoln told him that it was as good a reason as any. "Then what do you think would help her? Because as surely as we're sitting here, I know you have a plan."

"I do, as a matter of fact. Why don't we have a vendor shop? Where people could have a section of that big warehouse downtown that has been empty for years. They can display it any way they want, put out their things, and sell them. It wouldn't take much to get the place ready. A few pieces of tape to mark off the areas, after we clean it up, anyway. Then we find people that would fit in it and let them have at it." Lucas asked about rent. "Do we need to go there? I mean, for now, can't we just help the town out by letting them have a permanent place to sell some things for a little extra cash?"

"We'd have to have something, or we'll have people spreading out and there won't be room for anyone." He said he could see that too. "All right. How about we charge something like five bucks a square foot? That's not too much. A ten by ten space would be fifty bucks. And then if they have trouble making that, we could work something else out."

"I like that idea. Are you going to head it up?" Lucas pointed out that it had been his idea. "All right then, it'll give me something to do for the moment. Did you hear that Ginger took over the greenhouse project? I was glad to hand it over."

"I don't think she'll take on another for you, so you should really find someone else to put on it when you get it set up." He said he was good at starting it, just not long-term stuff. "Yes, I've realized that about you over the decades. Not to say that you don't have good ideas and they usually make us money, as well as others too. But you need to have a project manager that will take over when you get it organized."

"That's a great idea. Someone that I can trust, for sure. Thanks." As he started away after their meal, he turned back to his brother. "Watch out—Walton is on the loose, and they can't find him."

"I am. I've already put in extra security at the house Ginger is staying in, and I have all the right people at the greenhouse, grocery store, and daycare where Mattie goes." He thanked him. "You might want to think about getting your guard up too. With Grace being Ginger's twin, he might just be stupid enough to try and take her instead."

He'd not thought of that. And while they were similar

in features, they were nothing alike personality-wise. Ginger was like the girl next door. Grace was the one that joined a spitting contest and usually came out the winner. Lincoln would never tell her that, but that's the way he felt.

Chapter 6

Walton knew his family attorney's name, but not how to get in touch with him without getting into hot water. The newspapers, as well as the television news, were saying that he was armed and dangerous, and that if he was encountered, they were to not engage but to call the police.

"Armed and dangerous. I have a gun, yes, but I'm not dangerous." He hadn't killed his parents, as the news was saying. Nor did he bathe himself in their blood as the tabloids were plastering all over their front pages. He was just trying to get his son. "Okay, so I did *try* to kill Ginger and her daughter, but that wasn't dangerous to anyone but them, right?"

He had always been the type of person to talk to himself. Even when he was kid, he'd ask himself questions, work out the answers, and go with his thoughts. It had served him well over the years, and he thought that it was a good idea since he was much smarter than most of his friends. Hell, than most people because he worked things out before making a final decision.

The attorney for the family was hard to reach. He wasn't sure, first, the name of the firm that he worked for, just that it had a few names on their front door and he was one of them. Nor did he know what office the man might work at. That was important for him to know, because apparently, they didn't know where their employees were and expected the clients to keep tabs on them.

When he was going through his dad's wallet, he found not only more cash slipped behind the picture area, but also a business card. It had not just the firm's name, but also the man's. Howard Taylor even had his personal number on the back of the card. Walton thought about starting there but didn't want to piss the man off before he asked him a few questions.

"Mr. Conrad. I certainly didn't expect to hear from you. What is it I can do for you?" He said that he'd not killed his parents. "Yes, I'm aware of that. You mother did it. Murder-suicide is what it was. But you were there in the room when it happened, and the police would like to have a word with you. Not to mention, you're out of jail when you're not supposed to be."

"This has all been a mistake. I didn't do anything wrong. I know that I threatened Ginger, but I didn't hurt her. And she lied to me about the baby or I would have taken better care that he wasn't hurt." He asked about having her tied to the bed when he wanted to have intercourse with her. "How did you find out about that?"

"I've spoken to her, with her attorney present. Your father had some plans to help the girl leave the country soon." He asked why he'd do that. "I wouldn't know, sir. I was just your his attorney. What plans he had for the child, I don't know. And we'll never know now."

But Walton was pretty sure that he did know. And not only that, but whatever his plans were, they were still going to be executed. They were going to take his kid and sell it off, or have it killed. Rather than seeing him or his father raise it, they were going to take him out of his hands.

"I need to know when you're reading the will." He said that if his name was in it, he'd be notified. "What do you mean, if? I'm their only son, of course I'll be in it."

"Your father told you over and over that he was not leaving you a dime, Mr. Conrad. If your name is in the will, as I have said, then you will be notified by this firm. Until the police are finished with the crime scene and your poor parents are properly buried, you'll just have to wait, I'm afraid."

"How can I get some money until then?" Mr. Taylor asked where he thought it should come from. "My estate. My father has left it all to me as his only child, and I'd like to get some money from it so that I can live. The police are all over the house."

"With good reason, I'd say. Your mother slit your father's throat, then her own. And there you sat doing nothing for either but to steal from them both. Even your poor dead father; you took his wallet from him as he bled out. Have you no shame?" He said that he didn't when he was running. "I don't know what to tell you, young man. I would suggest that you turn yourself in before you get in any deeper. Barring that, I have nothing else to advise."

"Am I in the will?" He didn't answer him, but even that

was telling enough. "The son of a bitch took me out, didn't he?"

"Your mother inherited everything, since he died first. And yes, before you ask, there was a will for her as well. And again, once it's to be read, if you are in it, then you will be notified." He laughed a little and then spoke again. "Good day to you, Mr. Conrad. It's been a pleasure working with your family."

Then the line went dead. Like his father had done to him, the fucking little shit had cut him off. Walton had no idea what his mother would have done, but he could almost see his father standing over her while she signed where she was told. And there would be nothing in her will for him either. What a wonderful family he had.

Now he had to come up with a plan to make some cash so that he and little Walton could get out of the country. He was going to get his son, even if he had to kidnap him. As he sat there, thinking about that plan, something else occurred to him. Ginger would be able to get some cash from her sister.

Walton had read about how Grace was this big rising star when it came to some art shit. He supposed it was painting, since there was a big one right behind her in the picture. Another thing that no one had told him, Grace was the same as Ginger by looks. He could have had the stupid artist if he'd known, and there wouldn't have been any kid to be driving him crazy.

When he'd spotted Ginger a few years ago, she'd been working in a doctor's office. He'd taken one of his buddies there to get stitches removed or something. Anyway, she'd made him an appointment and then set him up with paperwork so that he could use her boss as his family doctor. There wasn't a damned thing wrong with him, but he wanted to see her again and again.

After three months of him coming in to see her all the time, she told him that she didn't want him coming into her place of business. He'd yet to get an address or phone number from her — she'd been real cagey about both.

But he was persistent, and he finally figured out where she lived by following her a few times. Even in that she was slick, not going directly to her home but stopping about a thousand places until she got there. He'd usually get bored with her shopping and leave. That was the only reason it took him so long to find her.

But she called the cops on him when he came to see her. That was when he found out Ginger had that kid. It took him another two weeks to get her to his house. That had been the most difficult time he'd had. The cops were all over her place, and the kid was always with her. He'd not meant to take it at all, but that was the only way. And because he'd been so pissed, he'd raped her hard and knew that he'd hurt her badly.

He'd not been able to take her to a regular doctor, but to see a friend of his that had almost graduated from college with a degree in animals. Something to do with them breeding; hell, he didn't know. Anyway, he gave her something for pain and she slept a lot and he had to deal with the brat.

Then she found his dragon.

Having her around wasn't so bad after that. A few times he had thought that the dragon had eaten her. Or crushed her. Whenever she was missing for a couple days he had

91

been thrilled about it. Then she'd turn up and he'd have to deal with her all over. Knocking her around didn't give him any satisfaction either—she would just stare at him without saying a single word. Fucking little shit.

As the days wore on and her mom got better, he saw less and less of the kid. He knew that Ginger was hiding her from him, and usually he'd not care. But when he wanted to bring Ginger in line for something, he used the brat to do it. Like letting him near her to fuck her.

She would fight him like he was going to hurt her. The least she could do was to put out since he was housing her and the kid and feeding them every day. But she fought every single time, and instead of getting old and turning him off, it did the opposite. That got to be so much fun that he wanted to fuck her nightly. And he did.

Then she told him she was pregnant. He wasn't sure how it hadn't happened sooner. The way he went after her, she should have been carrying his kid long before that. So, he figured that she'd done something before, and he tied her to the bed and then to the kitchen table when he was gone. She damned well wouldn't hurt that one.

Things had been going okay until the dragon got away and she lied to him about the baby's sex. That was when he decided to take care of his problem and kill them both. But that bitch in the mountain had interfered and he'd been arrested. Things went to shit after that.

Now here he was, in a cheap hotel trying to figure out what the fuck his father had done to him with the will. And if it was true about his mom inheriting everything, he had a feeling he was just as screwed that way too. While she might have loved him — who knew really, the way she acted all the time — she never went against his father.

"Well she did, didn't she? Cut his throat right open." He could laugh about it now, but when she'd done it, he could have sworn that she would go after him next. Then she'd cut her own instead.

The sound of screaming tires had him looking out the window. The four cruisers that he could see made him tense up, but not for long. Gathering all his shit, which wasn't that much, he made his way to the back of the room and out the window. Since he had figured this may happen, someone noticing him and calling in the cops, he'd made a getaway bag of things from the breakfast bar in the hotel, as well as some of their towels and toiletries. Also, he'd taken out the glass window.

He hit the ground running, grabbing the bag that he'd stolen a couple days ago as he ran to the woods. There wasn't much back here, and with all the foliage, he was able to hide well up within the trees. Twice the cops walked right by him, and both times he'd had to hold his breath. Knowing his area, like the forest behind the hotel, had just saved his ass.

While he was up there, he thought about what the hell he was going to do now. He needed cash, enough of it to get out of the country with an infant. Then he had to get little Walton and flee. Walton knew enough people that he could easily get out of the United States, but with a little kid, he hadn't any idea how to make that work.

"I'll cross that bridge when I come to it."

He had to get cash, and now, that was not only going to buy him passage, but grease a few palms while he was hiding.

93

Walton had a feeling that Mr. Taylor had kept him on the phone just long enough for him to get into trouble with the cops.

First things first. Get Ginger and his son so that he could ransom Ginger back to her sister for a tidy sum. How much that would be he was still working out, but it would be great sum, worthy of a famous or semi-famous painter.

~~~

Xavier looked at the three paintings that she had finished; well, at least those others knew about. One was of the wooded area behind their house with a mountain rising out of the trees. The second was of the lazy creek she'd encountered while walking in the forest one afternoon. And the final piece, which had been a work in progress of the castle that kept coming back to her, was finished finally.

The dragon had given her fits. She wanted it to look like one of the Manning men. She'd seen them all two nights ago when it had been raining and they went flying, and thought he'd be perfect for the setting. But Muse had other plans, apparently, and she had to let herself paint him the way he had said. And it turned out beautifully.

"This one is my favorite. Do you know where that castle is?" She said in her mind. "No, it's in Scotland. Lincoln owns it. Well, I guess you both do now. Did he tell you about it? Because you have it dead on from when I was there last. Even the drawbridge is perfect, with the design of the wood to make it look like the rest of the area."

"I've never seen the castle, but I knew that he had one." Xavier kept staring at it. "I wanted to see if they look all right for the next showing, because I don't want to go down this path if you think they're wrong."

"I think they're perfect. And I'd like to buy this one. No matter the price." She told him he could have it if it didn't sell. "Oh, it will. I bet it'll be the first that does if you don't let me buy it. If Garrett knows his stuff, which he does, then he'll be using this as a teaser on the flyers that go out."

"I have more." He turned and looked at her. "I've never seen a castle before. Ever. And suddenly, I'm painting medieval times with men in armor and dragons instead of horses. But the others, they're the same kind. I don't know why I painted them. But if you...I have some more."

"May I see them?" She wasn't sure that she wanted him to. She'd not shown them to anyone but Benson, and he'd told her they were good pieces. He wasn't much of a talker, that one. "I won't tell anyone if you don't want others to see them. I think you're wrong for not showing off your talent, but I'll abide by your wishes."

"It's not that." She asked him to follow her. "I'm glad that I have this canvas stretcher. I don't think I could have afforded a piece as large as this one is. And the fact that I've had to paint it while it's on the floor makes me think that it's all wrong. I'm babbling because I don't want you to tell me that it sucks."

"I'd be nicer about it than that, I'd hope." She pushed open the door to the large part of the barn that wasn't being used right now. There, lying on the floor, was her painting. "Holy Christ, Grace, it's magnificent."

There was another castle in the far left of the painting. It was still large in the scene, mostly because of the size of the canvas. But it was what was in the foreground that she was worried about. The men on horses, while several dragons, all different hues of blue, were just behind them. They were all looking up at the large dragon in the sky. A silver one that made her think of stars during midnight. Instead of looking at the painting again, she watched Xavier's face as he talked about what he was feeling and seeing.

"It's a cold morning, I can actually see the breath of the horses. And the dragons, warm-blooded as they are, the fog coming up off their bodies, are making a rain cloud just above them. These horses look like they could leap right out of the canvas, they're so realistic. They're simply beautiful in their stance and coloring. You have the muscle tone perfect for what sort of horses they are, as if they'd been carrying a great deal of weight for a long time." She asked if they looked like real horses. "Yes. Haven't you ever seen one before?"

"No. I mean, we, for the most part, lived in the city. Apartments. There was barely enough room around the area to have dirt that we could play in." Xavier turned and looked at her. "I've most definitely never laid eyes on a man in this sort of uniform. But I could see them, each with their full armor on and their faces muddy with blood and dirt. And the swords that they carried. They couldn't be dull with just a single blade that ran into the scabbard either. They needed to be marked. And what the markings mean I have no idea, but that was what I saw on them."

He stared at her for several minutes, and she thought for sure that he was trying to think of a way to tell her that she had it all wrong. That she was better off hiding this one. There wasn't any way that she was going to show him the others, not after he told her what a crappy painter she was.

"It's dragon. The words say, 'Death to all that rise up against the dragons of our clan. Long life to those who sacrifice themselves to serve the king of dragons.' You got every letter right, and it's beautiful." He looked at the painting again. "No human can speak the language you have there. Not even to write it out like you have."

She laughed, and he asked what was so funny. "The title of the painting. I had no idea what that said there, but the name of the painting is King of Dragons."

"Have you told anyone about this, love?" She told him that she'd only shown him. "This will go for big bucks, but you have to get permission from Cooper to sell it. I'm going to tell you that he'll want to buy it, simply because it's that good. Tell him that you want to display it at the show, but no one will get it but him if he offers you a good price. What else do you have? I know you have more. Where are they?"

"They're here too." She turned on all the lights and he wandered around the room. She didn't move this time, standing where she was while he took them in. "They're the battle after this scene here. Again, I don't know where this came from, but it was like I was possessed, and had to paint it. The blood...there is so much of it in the last one that it took me several days to get it right. It was as if Muse had been there and he wanted the story told."

"Have you ever had this happen to you before? When the muse wanted you to paint something so badly?" She told him not as hard, no. "So, since you came here, you've been painting this sort of venue? The medieval times."

"Yes. I don't even read that sort of books." He turned to her and smiled. It scared her a little. Like he'd figured it

97

out and was going to tease her with his information. "What? What is going on?"

"You are being guided by your muse, who is now a dragon, I think. I mean, it stands to reason that since we can never change you into one, that you'd have something that would be there with you all the time. And in this, your dragon is your muse now, and he's telling you his story." She asked how he'd come to that. "Because he's dead. See? This painting right here, the silver dragon has been slain. And he is the one guiding you to paint what you really have no knowledge of. It's the only way to explain that you could have known those words and that they were on the sword of the king that my father served. I hope you don't mind, but I've called my brothers here. They'll want to see this too."

"Tell them not to be mean to me, please." Xavier hugged her and kissed her on the forehead. It was what they all did to her. It was very sweet. But it made her no less afraid of what the others might say to her.

"Garrett is here too. He came to see Lucas on another matter, and he's with him. They're bringing up the rear." She nodded, thinking that she might as well get it over with about him telling her that it wasn't want he wanted. "Don't be so hard on yourself. These are going to be great."

Lincoln was the first to show up, and he loved the painting still on the easel. But when he came back to where his brother was, he was as silent as Xavier had become since telling her that the paintings were great. All the men, and the women too, stared at the one on the floor as if it was speaking to them. Much like it had to her while she was painting it. When they didn't say anything, she did.

"I don't know why I painted this. And so large. I'm not full of myself, if that's what you're thinking. But to get the detail in I needed it large. It's too big, isn't it? I suppose I could have broken it up like I did the others, but—"

She showed Garrett the others when he asked her where they were. The rest of them followed him around the room as he started with the second, smaller painting, and went around the room to the other twelve. Grace went into her studio and stood there looking at the blank canvas, hoping that this time she would be able to paint something that wasn't so out of her reach.

"I'll take them all." She turned and looked at Garrett when he spoke from behind her. "Christ, woman, you're going to be famous after this. No one is going to say anything about a painter without speaking your name in hushed tones. You outdid yourself to the point where I'm afraid that you will have outgrown my little gallery."

"I want the larger one." They were all arguing over the paintings. But Cooper was the loudest and the one that said he wanted it. "I'd take them all if I had the room. Hell, I don't even know what I'm going to do with that one. But I want it. It's magnificent." Her sister had joined them while they were looking, and she wanted to run away with her. "What will it take for me to buy that painting?"

"You'll let her display it at her next...no make it two showings?" Garrett was in money making mode, and she had to laugh. "Oh honey, this painting will be the envy of every being on this earth. Please tell me that you're going to paint like this forever."

"I don't know. As I was telling Xavier, Muse wanted

this done. He thinks that my muse has somehow been taken over by a dragon and he wanted his story told." Cooper said that he'd believe it. "I don't know what to believe. But these paintings, they were the easiest and the hardest things I've ever done."

"Do you think we could set it upright?" She said it was more than likely very heavy. Lincoln smiled and nodded at her. "Yes, I've no doubt, but I'd love to see it that way. I have a feeling that it's going to be even more spectacular than it is now."

It took all seven of them to set the painting up. Even Winnie helped with it, and once it was sitting against the wall, she had a thought that the frame was going to cost more than the painting would bring. She said that to Lincoln when he came to stand beside her.

"I think you're naïve if you think this will go for anything less than a million dollars." She looked at him, shocked. "I'm serious. I heard Garrett tell Cooper that he could have it for just over a million, but to the public, he was going to put three million on it. Just to generate interest in your work."

"A million dollars? Are you sure?" Lincoln nodded and kissed her. All she could think about was how much money that was. And she was sure that he'd gotten it wrong. There was no possible way that she had just sold a million-dollar painting.

Chapter 7

Lincoln was setting up his computer when he heard someone in the front hall. He could hear Grace speaking, but didn't know who to. When he got up, heading to the door when the voices got louder, he saw the other man before he noticed him. When he turned and looked after Lincoln cleared his throat, he knew who he was right away.

"You must be the stupidest man alive. What the hell are you doing in our home?" Walton looked at Grace, then back at Lincoln as he continued. "You know that you're a wanted man, don't you? You should be in jail, not hanging around as if you don't have a care in the world."

"I'm talking to my sister-in-law. You have no business interrupting." Lincoln pointed out that he hadn't married Ginger and never would. "You got that right, but I want to see my son. I know he's here sometimes. He's my kid, no matter what she says to the contrary."

"Ginger didn't list your name on the certificate?" Walton

101

said he didn't know, they didn't have a Conrad birth certificate on file. "I guess you didn't hear then. His last name is Rice. And good for her. I'd have advised her not to give yours as well. What do you want with Wendall?" He asked who that was. "Ginger's son is Wendall Rice."

"What the hell kind of name is Wendall? And why doesn't he have my name? This is why I should have him now. If she were to keep this up, he'd be the biggest dork in school. Just tell me where he is, Grace, and I'll be on my way." Grace said nothing, so Walton looked at him. "You can understand this, can't you? I bet you were called Abe your entire life because of your name."

"Actually, I was born well before he was, and always thought that he was named for me, not the other way around." At the look of confusion on his face, Lincoln laughed. "Don't hurt yourself, Walton. Also, your son is in good hands. And well cared for. Better than I'm sure a murderer would be able to."

"I didn't kill my parents." He didn't say anything. "My mom got up and did that all on her own. And then she murdered herself. I think she was just tired of living with my dad. I know that I was. He was a mean person. But I'm going to inherit soon, and I'll be able to have nannies out the ass for him and send him to the most expensive schools. He'll be a great kid. And mine."

"That isn't going to happen, Walton. My sister is doing a wonderful job of raising her son to be a good man. And you better stay away from her or else." He actually asked Grace or what. "I'll rain a hurt down on you that you'll feel for the rest of your very short life. I promise you, should you touch any of them, I'll hunt you down."

"Big words for such a little girl." He shoved her, and before he could move again, Lincoln had him by the throat and was tightening his grip. As he struggled, turning darker and darker all the time, he felt Cooper talk to him.

He's not worth it. The paperwork would be a killer. He told him that he'd hurt his mate. *She said that he only pushed her. And you're terrifying her. Let the jackass go and we'll deal with him in a more personal way.*

Instead of putting him down, he tossed him toward the wall. The crack he left said that he hit pretty hard, but the idiot stood right up. It wasn't two seconds before he was back on the floor and not moving. Grace jerked Lincoln toward her and then slapped him across the face.

"What was that for?" She told him. "I know that you can take care of yourself, but he touched you. And no one touches what is mine, Grace."

"I'm going to pretend that you didn't just go all Neanderthal on me." He grinned, and she asked if he wanted her to hit him again. "You're being an ass."

"Because I was protecting you?" He had gotten loud and tried to calm himself down. He wasn't mad, just shocked. "I love you, and he might have hurt you."

"Then you step in when he's about to hurt me. Not when I was just ready to kick him in the balls until they were right under his double chin." He couldn't help it, he laughed. "I'm not being funny."

"You're right, you're not the least bit funny." He laughed again. "I'm sorry, but I can see the look on his face when you would have done that. I think, for some reason, he has it in his head that you and your sister are helpless. You should have been able to prove otherwise to him. And for that, I'm profoundly sorry."

"Good." She stared at him and then turned to walk away. "Men. Why do they have to be so macho all the time?"

"Shall I call the police? I don't want that to be against your policy of taking care of yourself." She flipped him off and he had a good laugh about that too as he pulled out his cell. But when he turned around Walton was gone. He had no idea when that had happened, but he ran after Grace to make sure that he wasn't in the house.

"What is it?" She held him as he told her what happened. "He got up from that? Christ, he must have the luck of a cat, nine lives and all. You should have let me kick him. Men do not get up from that without a lot of complaining."

He kissed her again then called the police. Lincoln did leave out the part where he'd gotten into trouble with his mate about how to take care of Walton, and they said that they'd send a car right over. Lincoln wasn't sure that he'd not hurt Walton badly, and the fact that he got up and took off made him think he was on drugs. He tried to remember if he'd smelled them on him and couldn't.

Once they were on site he let them ask the questions. There was something about this whole thing that made him think that Walton had come by for another reason than just to see his son. And how did he know that he was here sometimes? Was he stalking them? Was Grace safe in the studio? Was Ginger at the greenhouse? He decided they needed to have a family meeting, just to make sure that they were all keeping tabs on each other. And if Grace didn't like it, he'd beat her bottom and tell her he was going to be all manly. He might even do that anyway—it sounded like fun. He told her his plans.

"Have them come for dinner. We've not had them all here since we moved in." He told Grace that was an excellent idea. "Also, have Ginger bring the kids. I'll feel better about them staying here rather than at the house alone. I know you have it guarded, but I'd prefer if he wasn't able to trap her someplace with them."

"I'll have the staff ready some of the rooms for them. I think there might even be a baby bed from the pack that we can use." The phone was ringing when she went to the kitchen to tell Finny they were having guests and see what they could have. He answered the phone. "Lincoln Manning, may I help you?"

"Mr. Manning, my name is Howard Taylor. I'd like to speak to you if I may. I'm to understand that you're married to Grace Rice, sister of Ginger. She's the one I'm trying to get ahold of. There is some.... A change was made to the will of Mrs. Conrad, and I need to discuss it with her."

"Sure. If you can make it this evening, her and the children are going to be staying here while they hunt for Walton." He said that was an excellent idea. "He was here earlier threatening my wife, and he wants to see the little boy."

"Don't let him do that, please. I have it on good authority that he plans to leave the country with him. He wishes to raise it as his own." The man laughed. "He isn't stupid, not book wise at least, but he's bragging that he has a son and will be raising him to be a lot like him. He's also been to the courthouse looking for a birth certificate. Ms. Rice did the correct thing by not naming him as the father."

"Finding out Wendall's name seemed to upset him." Lincoln laughed a little. "We'll all be here about six. I'm sorry though, but we'll have to see identification when you arrive. I don't want anything else to happen to my family. I'm sure you understand."

"Oh yes, I do. I'll see you soon. Thank you, Mr. Manning." He told him it was Lincoln. "Yes, all right. And please call me Howard."

As Lincoln made his way back to his offices, he wondered what had changed in the will. And if that was why she'd killed her husband first. From what he was to understand about the woman from those that knew the couple, she barely said a word and was under the rule of her husband. Lincoln didn't think that Grace would ever bow before him as the older woman had in her marriage. And he was sure that he didn't want her to. That wasn't the way to have a life with someone that you loved.

Getting his computer set up only took about ten minutes. But he had so many boxes in the room that he decided to unpack the books as well as the many things he'd collected over the years to put on the shelves. There wasn't a great many considering how old he was, but the items were beautiful to him. He looked up when Grace entered.

"I just got off the phone with Garrett." She began unwrapping things and setting them on the shelf too. "He said he's sending over a mockup of a flyer and wants to know if I'd go for an extra night with the showing. I told him it didn't matter to me."

"We'll get a hotel." He could tell she was distracted and

tried to get her out of the mood. Finally, he gave up and asked her what happened.

"He did sell Cooper the painting. But he wouldn't pay the price." Lincoln was pissed then, just like a fire had been set under him. He was reaching for his cheap ass brother when she continued. "Cooper said he'd only pay the full price, like the public would have. Why would he do that?"

"I don't know, love. Perhaps you could ask him yourself." She nodded. "If you don't mind my asking, how much did he pay for it? And just so you understand, he can well afford it. We all have more money than we can ever spend."

"Three point seven million. I don't understand that." Lincoln asked her what. "First of all, why someone would pay that much for a painting by a virtually unknown artist, and why everyone thinks all of them will sell like that one did."

"Can I ask you something first?" She nodded as she sat down when the box was empty. "When you painted that first picture, the one on the large canvas, what did you think was going to happen to it? And honestly, what did you want to?"

"I really never thought beyond getting it done so that I could move onto the next, and then the next after that. It was like if I didn't paint them, I'd die or something." He nodded, understanding the need to finish a project once it was started. "I have to tell you something, I have the same feelings about more that I want to do. This time it's not dragons, but wolves. The first is so complete in my head that I could literally just go paint it without thinking about it."

"Then you should. And yes, I think that every piece will sell." She said that she'd have to wait until tomorrow, the canvas needed to be stretched. "I can help with that. I've done that sort of work before. Is it going to be as big as the King painting?"

"I don't think so. It'll be large, but manageable for me. The other was difficult to paint because I had to come up with ways to get to the center of it. With this one, I'll be able to walk around it. It would be easier if it were upright, but I'd not be able to paint without a ladder or scaffolding."

He would see about getting her what she needed. Lincoln wasn't going to have anything stand in her way while she worked. Christ, three million. He was going to have to tell Cooper he got off cheap, just to tease him. But he did wonder if the wolf painting would be about an old battle as well. Hank would know as soon as it was finished. He might even buy it.

~~~

Howard had never had a meeting with such large men before. He always thought that he was taller than the average male, but they towered over him. And the women—well, it was clear to him who ran the family. The men would have laid down their lives for these ladies.

"Did you get plenty to eat, Mr. Taylor?" He told Ginger that he had, and for her to call him Howard. "All right. And I'm Ginger. They said that you wanted to speak to me. If you need to make it private, that's fine, but I'm going to tell them all anyway. So, if you don't mind, I'd like to know what the Conrad estate has to do with me."

"As I was telling your brother-in-law, Mrs. Conrad changed her will a few weeks before she killed herself. And in it, she must have known about you, your daughter, and son. She didn't know what sex your baby was, but she was heartbroken that it was Walton's child. She said in the will that she hoped you did a better job of raising your child than she did hers." Ginger looked as if she was going to cry, and he handed her his handkerchief. "She was a troubled woman, my dear. Her husband was abusive. Not physically, but verbally. He was forever telling her what a fool she was, that she was stupid. And Walton wasn't any better. The day that she murdered her husband must have been the most difficult thing she'd ever done. But in reading the will, which I'll get to, I think I understand a great deal better why she did it."

"Please, let's hear it, if you don't mind." He nodded and pulled out the will. He asked if it was all right if he just skipped to the meat of the thing. "Yes, if you think the rest is unnecessary. I don't understand why you think I'd need to know this."

She took the part he pointed out for her. When she began reading it to herself, the others asked if she could share. Ginger began again aloud, and he knew this was going to be a tear jerker.

"To my darling grandchild. First, I want to tell you how sorry I am that I cannot be there for you as a grandma. I would like you to remember me fondly, and to not judge me too harshly. I did what I needed to do to survive. And I didn't even do that very well. I would like to tell you a shortened version of my life.

"I met your grandfather when I was eighteen. I was stupid, I know that now, in thinking that I could change him into a man I could love. But he never wanted my love. Only the prestige and money I brought to the marriage. Then a few months later, my own parents died, leaving me with a

109

multimillion dollar estate. As you can well imagine, Walton was happy. I was not.

"The money became a sore spot for us. I had it, he didn't. And no matter how many times he begged, beat, or even tried to kill me for it, I would never sign it over to him. And for that, I paid the price. I became the world's loneliest rich person.

"Just recently he brought me a will and told me to sign it. It had in it that he was going to inherit all my estate and the houses that I owned. I didn't sign it. And as you can well imagine, I suffered for it. But enough about that. I had this drawn up in the hopes that you could use the money for goodness and kindness. To bring to your home a love that I have never had. A friendship with people you enjoy, and money so you may enjoy a life that I wished I had had. You deserve it, simply because you are my grandchild, despite the problems you will encounter with your father."

Ginger looked at him when she read down to the bottom of the page. She was confused, he could see that, but he waited for her to ask questions. He was sure she would have plenty.

"She left my son her estate." He said that she did. "Why did she do that? I mean, she doesn't know me from anyone."

"Molly was a very smart woman. She did manage to keep her money, even though throughout her marriage to Walton it became difficult. And she also turned her millions into more, without his knowledge, or mine for that matter. Molly might have given someone the illusion that she was a beaten woman, when all along she was plotting and planning better than any of us could have imagined." Ginger said that she was sorry for her. "I am as well. I never got to know the woman that she truly was. Walton was a smart man too, but he was ignorant to the needs of his wife. And after their son started to cause them trouble, he cut him out of the will too. His plan, according to the will that Molly wouldn't sign, was for all her money to go to him. And in the event, which he never believed would happen, that she outlived him, then it would go to several charities he liked and supported. Walter the son would get nothing. Nor did Molly leave him anything."

"Will she need to do anything to get the money for her son?" He knew Cooper would want to get to the nitty gritty of things. Howard told him what he knew to happen now. "So, she doesn't have to claim it publicly or anything. I can't help but think that would be a bad idea."

"Yes, I agree. And it's set up so that Ms. Rice can manage the estate as she wishes and spend any money that she wants. Molly wanted her to be happy as well, and to have the ability to have fun. Something that she wasn't able to do." Howard asked if she wanted to know her family's net worth. When she nodded but held onto her sister, he had to smile. She was going to be shocked. "In addition to all my worldly possessions, I leave all my homes to the unborn, or at this time born, child of Ginger Rice. I also leave her the house in town, as well as the many others that were left to me from my parents' estate. There is cash and jewelry in a safety deposit box that will be opened upon her request, any and all items listed below can be sold at any time should she wish it. I will not hold any kind of stipulations over anyone as was done to me."

"You're saying there is more than just the house in town?" He said there's a total of nine, some in several different countries. "Really? Wendall has nine homes."

She said it like a question, but he assured her it was right.

111

Then he told her the amount of money. Just over two billion dollars, not including the residences or the items inside them. When she didn't speak, he asked if she was going to faint.

"I'm made of sterner stuff than that, sir." He told her he was sorry but had to bite back a laugh. "Walton, he won't get any of this? He doesn't have any rights to this money or the houses at all, correct?"

"No, none of it. The will is legal, and since she outlived her husband by a few minutes at best, then his estate, which isn't nearly as much, went to her as well. That too is mentioned here for you. It's just under one million." He watched her carefully when she got up to pace. "There is more if I can go on."

"You could, sir, but I don't think I'd hear a single word of it. I'm overwhelmed and terrified of all this." He said he understood. "Do you? I was dirt poor when I met my husband. Then he died, and I was even poorer. But we had love and loved well. Then this monster comes along and nearly kills me, then ties me to his bed and gives me a son. Now his mother is giving us the world. I think I misspoke. I'm more than overwhelmed. I can't even think of a word to describe how I'm feeling."

"I'm sorry about all of this. But I would like to tell you that so long as you live, you'll never have to worry about money again. There is also a trust fund set up for Mattie. When you have time, you need to contact the attorney in charge of that. I'm only here today because my friend, the man who set this up, passed away this morning." She told him she was sorry. "I am as well. It was his fondest dream to see the estate taken care of, and he didn't get to do what he wanted for you. I had no idea until he called me last night, telling me he wasn't feeling well, and asked if I could do this for him. And then he was gone."

Howard answered the questions put to him. He had gone over the file twice to make sure that he'd not missed anything, and then familiarized himself with the estate. There was more to it, but he knew for now it was enough that she understood she was a wealthy woman. Howard was sure the Mannings would help her more than any attorney could.

As he was leaving the home, he thought about young Walton. He was skating on very thin ice if he messed with these men. It was rumored that they were dragons. Howard didn't know about that, but he did know they were men of worth. They were also richer than Ms. Rice by a great deal. He knew that she was going to be just fine.

Stopping at the town's only light, he felt the sting of something hitting him in the face. He looked around, wiping at something running over his cheek. There he stood, Walton Conrad, with a gun pointed right at him. Reaching for his phone, he took several pictures and sent them to the first number that came up. The second shot took his breath away when it hit him in the chest. He was going to die. Howard should have known Walton would be pissed and come after him. Well, it was too late now.

"You mother fucker, where is my money?" He was dying anyway, so he told him to fuck off. Blood poured from his mouth as he spoke. "I want you to tell me where it is. You never called me."

"I told you...I would if your name was mentioned in her will." He asked him whose will he was talking about. "Your mother's. I told you all this."

"You said that you'd call me, and you didn't. I want to know what my father's will said." Howard was fading fast, but wanted to keep the young woman safe, so he said only that Molly had outlived his father and it was all hers. "But she's dead too. What did my mother leave me? Dad would have taken care of me."

"They both left you nothing. You were never mentioned in either will." The shot hit him in the shoulder, like he was trying to prolong this act he was a part of. "Killing me won't get you anything but a longer sentence. You have to know that."

"What I know is you cheated me out of the estate. Are you keeping it all for yourself?" He said that he got only his fees. Howard was no longer hurting, but he was weak. "Where is my money?"

"I keep telling you there isn't any, Walton. Your parents set up their wills so that you got nothing regardless of what order they died." He closed his eyes then, thinking this was the end. The next bullet hit him in the chest again, and he didn't even have the strength to touch the wound. He looked at his cell phone when it started ringing.

"They're coming for you, Walton." Howard coughed up blood and it poured from his mouth and nose. "They're going to send you away for the rest of your fucking life."

He aimed the gun again, and Howard never felt it enter his head.

Chapter 8

Grace walked through the house with her sister. It was huge. And she thought museums would have been jealous of the things inside it. When Ginger turned to her, she thought she was going to tell her that it was perfect.

"I hate this place." They both laughed. "I mean, besides the fact that Walton and his parents lived here. Look at all this stuff. What the heck were they going to do with it? Watch it grow older? And it's so crowded too. No room to move."

"This is only the first floor; maybe it'll get better." Like her, she no more believed that than the tooth faerie. Although, she'd have to check on that one. Who knew there were unicorns? Not her, that's for sure.

The rest was as bad if not worse. The master suite had so many dressers in it that she wondered if they were ever used. But a quick peek into a couple told her that each held a specific color for the man. One was filled with blue socks, shirts, and handkerchiefs. Another with gray. Not to be confused with a shade or two of darker gray in a separate dresser. And she noticed, there was nothing of Molly's.

It was obvious which room was hers as soon as they walked in. There was a single dresser, a closet full of dresses of beautiful colors, as well as hats. She must have loved to wear them, because Grace thought there could have easily been over a hundred. Some in boxes, others in plastic. And they matched the dresses too. Her heart broke once again for the sad woman.

"I can't live here. Could you?" Grace told Ginger that it wasn't for her to decide. "I'm not asking that. Would you?"

"Oh, hell no." They laughed again, but her sister did sit on the bed. "I'm guessing you're going to sell it all."

"Yes, but not like it is. I want to have an auction. This stuff must be worth something to someone. I wouldn't know how to go about it, but I'm sure one of the Mannings do." She said she was sure they'd been around long enough to invent it. "I still can't believe that this is all real. I've never had money. Now we have more than we could ever hope to spend. But that doesn't mean I'm going to be stupid with it. I don't want to end up in a ditch after all this."

"You? Never. You're the most frugal person I know. Not to mention, I think you are the smartest as well. You'll be keeping books of your books before you know it." She sat on the bed with her. "You don't mind living with us until we get Walton out of the picture, do you?"

"I love it there. And Lincoln is so good with the kids." She looked at her. "Are you going to have any?"

"No. I mean, we can't since I'm human and he's a dragon. Because of how they became, they'd need to be born in an

116

egg. We'll adopt, but I can't have his child. Carson was able to get pregnant because of some magic given to her. I'm not even sure how that would work."

"You two will make great parents. I know it. And any child that comes into your life will be so lucky to have you." She hugged her. "Okay, this house is toast, and we need to get rid of this crap. I cannot believe that man had that many suits. Did he wear one every day for a year? Whatever. What do you think I could do with them?"

"I was just thinking that you could donate them to the local shelter. There might be someone that could use one for an interview or something. The shirts too. I don't know about the socks—I guess the same thing. I don't know, maybe someone could cut them down and make rag runs out of them for every house in the county." Ginger laughed again. "It's been so long since you seemed this happy. I'm so pleased for you and the children. You're finally getting all that you deserve."

"Thanks. It's because of you." She asked how that was even possible. "You gave me the strength to go on after all that with Walton. And you looked for me so hard, I know you did. How were you to know that I was right under your nose with that monster?"

"The police were so sick of seeing me. I think I was there nearly every day to ask about you. Getting away like you did, that might have saved both you and the children's lives. I'm so grateful to Winnie, too, for getting you to safety after Wendall was shot." Grace hugged her sister tightly again. "I don't know what I'd do if you weren't around for me to hug when I want."

"Okay, enough of this. Let's get this place emptied, then sold. I'm perfectly happy with the house that I have, and I'll use the money from this to pay back Lincoln for the one that I'm in. And if he doesn't allow me to do that, then I'm going to move and take his niece and nephew with me." Grace told her that she'd make him take it then. "I knew you would. Okay, how about lunch? You can buy, because I'm just too wealthy to carry around cash."

They were still laughing when they got to the bottom of the stairs. Just as they were headed to the front door, it started to rattle. While she didn't have a definite idea who it might be, she had a feeling that it was Walton. He would have seen her car out front.

"Go back upstairs and hide." Ginger said she wasn't leaving her. "Yes, you will. You have those babies to care for and...and I'm an immortal."

"Well, that does trump me. All right, but if you get hurt, I'll never forgive you." She told her she wouldn't either. "Call out to the men. I'm pretty sure you can do that too."

"Winnie. I need Winnie." And almost as if she was standing there all along, she was with them. "We're in deep shit here. Can you help us?"

"Sure, but I really think she should do this herself." They both looked at Ginger, then back at the door when the windows at the side of it rattled. "You can do this. I'll be right here with you should it turn out badly. And, so you know, you're as much an immortal as the rest of the Mannings. You just have to not get shot in the heart."

"Well, I don't know about you two, but I'd really like not to." Ginger looked at her then started down the stairs, still talking. "I'm a fool. An idiot. I'm actually going down there and talk to a bigger idiot. What the hell is wrong with me?"

Grace looked at Winnie. "Don't let my sister be hurt. Please?" Winnie promised her that she wouldn't and went to the door too. Grace didn't have any idea why she was doing this and thought she should get her head examined. This was insane.

Ginger opened the door just as she stood beside her. Walton glanced at her, then drew back his fist to hit her. One of them anyway, but all he did was stand there when Ginger spoke.

"I'm not afraid of you any more, Walton. You hurt me once; you hit me this time, and I will stop at nothing to kill you." He looked like he might have believed her and put his fist down. "What do you want?"

"Besides into my home? I want my son. Where is he? And don't think you'll go unpunished for lying to me about him." She lifted her chin, and in that moment, Grace knew her sister had this. "What are you doing here anyway? This is my family home."

"It's mine. All of it. And *my* son's. We've decided to sell it all, however." Walton started forward. Grace wasn't sure what his intentions were, but almost as soon as he took a step, he took one back. Then another. Winnie had stepped behind Ginger, and he was afraid of the other woman. "What's the matter, Walton? You afraid of women? Have you decided that we might not be as helpless as you thought?"

"Yeah, you're really brave when you have someone to help you, aren't you, Ginger? Well, I want you to mark my words—I don't know how you got my home, but I'll get it back. And my son too." She stared him down, and when he moved to leave, Grace decided that she didn't care for being brave, she wanted her mate with her. And his big assed dragon. But when he turned back, Walton looked mean. "I'm coming for you, Ginger. And we'll have a grand old time."

The sirens could be heard then, and he looked toward the road before smacking his fist to his hand and then taking off. She was going to keep an eye on the asshole just to make sure that he didn't come in the back door or something. As soon as the cruiser came into the yard, Winnie took over. She was directing them to where he went and what he'd said. Ginger just collapsed on the floor.

"You did really well." Ginger shook her head. "No, you really did. When he was about to hit you, you could have knocked me over when you told him off. I'm very proud of you, Ginger. You stood up to your bully."

"If he could have seen my knees, he'd have seen just how afraid of him I was. Oh, Grace, he wants Wendall. What if he gets past us and hurts him?" Grace told her that he didn't want to, just her. "Well, that's comforting. But you're right. I need to keep the kids out of harm's way. I don't know how yet, but they're the ones he's going to target from now on. Don't you think?"

"Yes. He'll go for the weakest. But if he gets to Wendall, he'll leave the rest alone, I believe." Winnie joined them on the floor. She looked...well, she strangely happy. "What have you done?"

"Why is that the first thing out of everyone's mouth? Okay, I did do something, but it was for the good of the family. They're not going to find him because I don't want

120

them to." Ginger asked why not. "Because he is going to be dealt with by the family of dragons. And that will get him out of our lives permanently."

"You mean they'll kill him." Ginger looked at her, then back at Winnie. "You know what? I don't care how so long as he is gone. I don't want to live the rest of my life looking over my shoulder. And even in jail, I don't trust that he'd leave us alone."

"I want you to have someone with you at all times. This is Sky. She is a faerie of considerable age and power. She will be with you for the rest of your days, but especially during this time with Walton." Ginger nodded to the little faerie. Grace's own were there as well, sitting on her shoulders. "Trust her enough to do what she tells you at all times. If she says run, do it like your life depends on it. If you're told to climb a tree, I want you to be assured that it's the best course of action for you. All right?"

"Yes. But will she be hurt with this? I don't want anyone else hurt because of Walton." Winnie told her that Sky was an earth faerie and could call upon it to help them both. "That didn't answer my question, but I'm assuming she can protect all of us because of that."

"Yes, and your children will each have a faerie as well. And know that they'll kill whatever comes after them with ill will. And that includes taking them from you." Ginger nodded. "Trust me, Ginger, you're going to be just fine. We're a family that takes care of its own."

As they drove home, Ginger was very quiet. Grace wasn't sure if she was thinking or in shock. Sky sat on her sister's lap and watched her. It was kind of creepy at first, but she had a feeling that she was getting to know her through a mind thingy. There was too much going on for her to be figuring out the mind of a faerie too.

~~~

Sadie watched the young man sneak around the property. She wasn't worried about him but enjoyed his attempts at being quiet. He was making more noise than it would take to wake the dead. He was a distraction for her though, so she put him to sleep. It would only last a few hours, but that was enough time for her to think about her dragons.

She so missed Coop. He'd been a good king, and a better leader than she'd ever worked with. His son was becoming the same. They were all good men and Coop would be proud of them.

Coop had come to her in desperation one night. He had told her of the things that he'd felt were going to happen. She had known he was right, but didn't want him making rash decisions. His lady wife had only just been murdered.

"I'm not being rash, my lady." He was the only one that had ever called her that. "I wish to make it so that my sons will be able to live among the humans. They will need this, or they'll be killed and butchered as their mother was."

"But to walk with the humans every day, Coop, will take some powerful magic. More than I have." He nodded and sat down on the floor. He was much too large for the only chair that she had. "I can work on something to keep them hidden, but that's the best I can do."

"I give you all that I am." She backed away from such power and told him to be serious. "I have never been more than I am right now. You may take my body and do with it as you please. The magic alone will do for you what no one else can. You and I both know that even should I give some other witch my magic, then it would be for naught. You are the strongest and kindest I know. I give this to you."

"Let me work on something." He told her this was all that he wanted. Coop said that he wanted his sons safe. "It will take me a few days to get what I will need, Coop. Just give me until the next full moon."

The month hadn't been nearly enough for her to work out something else to save the children of the dragon king. And no matter what she tried, it wasn't strong enough for them to be safe. It had to be his way, or it would never save them.

The morning of the full moon brought him to her door again. It was getting worse than it ever had. A dragon was being murdered every day. Even his brother's wife had been killed, along with their three children. Coop had been right— it was getting too much for a dragon not to walk with the humans.

"I have tried all that I could to make it work." He said that he knew she would. "There is a meeting with the dragons tonight. We'll practice the words here, then when the it's over and they're still lingering around, we'll borrow some of each of their magic, so that you'll be able to do this. I shall give you mine too, then hide away for some time to recuperate."

"I cannot thank you enough for this, my lady. My children will know what a kind and wonderful—"

"Nay, no one can know what has happened here today. You may tell them that I helped, but not what you have given me. I will, I promise, bring it back to them once they are at a stage in their lives they can handle it." He agreed with her and handed her a thick leather-bound book. "What is this? Is this the book of dragons?"

"No, a family history if you may. Words that would be to them and them alone. I wish for you to give it to Cooper when he's king. He'll not thank you, I think, for I tell him all, but he'll understand what we did here this night." She told him she'd do it. "Thank you, Sadie. You have saved my family, and for that, I give you all that I am."

They practiced through the day. And when he had it, she made him do it more. There could be no mistakes on this. He would kill his sons if this didn't go as planned. But she had confidence in him to do the right thing. Coop's children would be the very first shifters of their kind. Perhaps the only.

"They'll not be able to breed should they find their mate is a human." He said that he understood that, but they'd still find love. "Yes, I believe they will. They'll be handsome humans, as their dragons are. Are you sure about this, Coop?"

"Yes, as sure as I am about anything in the world. I want them to have a life without fear. Without someone hunting them down like animals. I want them to find a love like I had with their mother. A life full of wonder and fun." He was such a good man, and Sadie had wondered if the children would be as well.

They were that and better, she thought as she rocked in her chair. Soon she'd have to see Cooper and his brothers. After this mess with the man was finished. A wave of her hand and he was up again but headed home.

Sadie watched her soup on the fire as she thought of what to say to the young dragon. She knew that he had no liking for her. But she was all right with that. In their head, she was sure

124

that it was her fault their father was gone from this world. Her only hope was that the book would be helpful to them, and they'd be able to forgive her.

It was in her own heart that she had murdered their father. The magic that he'd given her had been put aside for Cooper, and someday she wanted to give it to him. Sadie, however, wasn't sure, but she thought Cooper much stronger than his father had been, and a good deal more handsome too. Smiling, she had the spoon near the pot stir it some more.

In a few days she knew that the man out there would try and kill the woman and her daughter. She wasn't clear on how that would happen, but she knew that he'd die a horrific death; not that he didn't deserve it. His father hadn't been much of a man, so it only stood to reason that the son wouldn't be either. Not raised the way he'd been. Too much and too little, she thought. Too much freedom and not enough discipline. That's what made a man into what Walton Conrad was.

When her pot was finished, she got up to serve herself. Soup was the best thing she could make, using the herbs and wild items that grew in the mountain. As she sat at her table, having put out her crackers that she hoarded like they were gold, she gave a little to the goddess of the earth before taking her first bite.

The earth called to her, much like the wind would a bird to come join them. She was ready to quit this earth and join her sisters in death. Life, the way that she'd always dreamed of it, was harder than she had expected. Fulfilling, yes, but difficult to do. She wasn't complaining, not much anyway, but she was tired and wanted to just lie down and let the earth take her into it. It was the way they did things, the witches of her time. The earth at her bare feet let her know that she was to have a visitor soon, and she wasn't surprised to find Winnie there.

"I've come to ask a favor of you." She looked at the faerie and then back at her soup. "You're as stubborn as you've always been, aren't you?"

"I am. But isn't that sort of you calling me yourself? I've never met a more stubborn woman than you. Faerie or not." She looked at her and smiled. "It is good to see you, Winnie. Or should I be calling you something more?"

"Winnie is fine. This favor I ask of you, it's not going to be something that you want, my trade for it." She asked her what she had in trade. "Me."

"Nay, I do not want you. You're too old and stubborn, as I have said. Teaching you to heed to my demand would be too taxing to a witch as old as me." She looked at her soup again. "I'll do the favor if you help me to talk to the young king."

"Now there is a stubborn person. He is not so set in his ways as he used to be. I think we have Carson to thank for that. But Cooper is his father's son, that's for sure." She told her that she'd been thinking the same. "I'll help you with him. I think that for as much as he blusters, he is curious as to what you have for him. But I'd wait on this other thing first."

"The young man who seeks his child?" Winnie said that was it. "He will come to his own on this. The child will be safe."

"Thank you." She told her that it wasn't her, but the others. "I figured that it would be something that the family would be a part of. But he will hurt her, given the chance. I'd like you to give the children a little extra, just to keep them safe. I can see that he tries to take them, but I don't know if they come to any harm."

"They do not." Again, Winnie thanked her. "I should ask you a few things too, while you are here. When you came to be the mate of the Manning dragon, did you get anything extra? The reason I ask is that I thought you powerful beyond what you had when I first met you. And even then, you were very strong in your magic."

"My parents are dead, you know that, correct?" She did and didn't waste her breath telling the woman that she was sorry. "When they were taken care of by the Manning family, I got some then. But as for mating to the big dragon, I got nothing more. Hudson did. A lot that he is still dealing with."

"You have more. Perhaps you just haven't figured it out yet." Winnie said that could be it, but she didn't know. "I'll put a spell around the children, but as I have said, they are protected very well now. I am intrigued as to how you would be giving yourself to me. I am a witch of considerable power. What would I want with a faerie and her powers?"

"You plan to join the rest of your kind in the earth." The girl was much too smart for her own good, and she told her so. "Thank you, but that is the truth. And I wish you all the happiness you can find from such a thing. But I can help you."

"How? There is no point in me denying what I want. I'm older than even you, though not by much." Winnie only smiled at her, also showing her all that she was. "Every time I see you thusly, I am amazed at the beauty of one like you. You are the most gorgeous creature ever created, I think. Now, tell me what you can do for an old woman such as me."

"I can ensure that you have a beautiful faerie garden in the glen not far from here. You will never be disturbed while resting, nor will your plot of land ever be bothered by the humans." It was a grand gift she was giving her. And one that Winnie could do too. "I will also tell of how you saved the dragons, which you have, and that even your great magic couldn't save Coop, the first of the Manning dragons."

"Such a gift for a bit of magic. Why would you do such a thing for me?" Winnie smiled at her again with a little flutter of her wings. And with that, a dusting arose, and she stared in wonderment.

"Long ago, before there were too many humans and while the skies were filled with dragons, a witch, just out on her own, came upon a child and gave a little of herself to save her life. The life that would later be able to give her a dying wish." She told her that she didn't know what she was speaking of.

The dust changed then, to the said little girl with her guts hanging out, her face full of fear and pain. And there beside her was a great dragon, one that she had, all alone, brought to justice. Sadie reached out to touch the child, thinking to give her comfort in her dying hour, only to feel the magic that would someday be used to bring the dragons to their fullest. Sadie was the witch, Winnie the small child.

"Had you not come upon me that day, I would surely have died. I know now what you saw when you touched me, and you could have taken all that I ever would have been with that help. But you saved me and gave me the strength to go on. For that, I would lay down my life for you, however short it would be." Sadie nodded, too touched to form words. "I promise you, on my oath as a faerie, I will protect you well after you die. For this, I owe you forever."

Chapter 9

Lincoln watched Mattie as she talked to her brother. He was resting in the crib next to the table while Ginger made the little girl and Lincoln something to eat. He had told her that he could fix his own meal, but she said it was no trouble and he let her. There was something going on with her and he could wait her out.

"Here you go, Mattie. Remember what I told you." Mattie nodded and looked at him. When he winked at her, she tried her best to do the same, blinking both eyes at the same time. He told her that she'd get it someday. "Lincoln, I need your help."

"I'm at your service. Just tell me who I have to slay and they're as good as gone." She smiled and handed him a large plate of food. "Is this about Walton? I told you, we have that covered."

"No. It's about the house and all the things that go with it. I need someone to give me an estimate on how much it would cost to auction it all off." He told her that he knew a couple people that could help. "Good, the sooner the better."

"If you don't mind me asking, Ginger, why are you in such a hurry? Are we not making you feel welcome?" She started to cry but stood from the table she'd only just sat at to turn her back to him. "I'm sorry. Did I do something to upset you?"

"No. I just want this finished. Something done that I can say, 'Well, that's off my list.' It feels like I've been on the run forever, and I want some stability in my life. For a little while, anyway. I have two children that I'm going to have to raise by myself. I have a job, not that I need one, but I want to do something for myself. And having that ugly over done house, off my list will be just the start for me." He nodded, waiting for the rest. "There was a time when I would have put up with a home like that, simply because it would have been security and safety for us. Now I find that I want to make my own decisions, not have them handed to me on a platter. The money is going to be helpful, don't get me wrong, but I need to do something productive."

"Then might I suggest that you have someone go in and appraise the things in there. Grace told me that it was a lot of old stuff, furniture and such." She nodded and told him how the master bedroom had several dressers. "Yes, he was a pompous ass. But he was a man who liked to look good. And match too, I guess."

He got her to laugh, and that was the point, he supposed. But he told her that he'd call a friend and have him come out to look. Lincoln asked if she'd sell it to him if it came to that.

"Yes, whatever it takes. I'm not sure that I'll be able to

live there after it's empty, but I need to know I'm making that happen for myself." He told her he understood that. "When Grace and I were there, I saw a couple small things I'd like to keep for Wendall. They were his grandmother's. I didn't take them when we left because Walton showed up. But if you go with your friend, could you please put them aside for me?"

"Yes, and I think you're very smart for not going with him alone. Walton is still a problem, and until he's taken care of, we'll keep an eye on you." She smiled and he could see the relief in her eyes. "What else may I do for you? This knight in shining armor stuff is kind of fun."

"You're more the dragon than the slayer, Lincoln." He laughed with her. "Oh, you have no idea how much better I feel just getting something started."

"I can see that. I'll give him a call now and we'll see when he can come out." She nodded, telling him how grateful she was that he was taking such good care of her sister. "She takes care of me more, Ginger. And I love her very much."

"And she loves you too. I have never seen her so happy before. And she's less tense too." Her face heated up red. "I'm sorry. I've not been out in a long time, and have been hanging around Grace too much. I've forgotten how to be a person."

"I think you're just perfect, and I'm glad to have you here." He got up and kissed her on the forehead. "You leave this to me. I was looking for a project, and you handed it to me. I need to keep busy. An idle dragon is one that is going to be in trouble."

"I have a feeling you would even if you were busy all the time." She picked up her son and sat down to nurse him. He started to leave her to it when she called him back. "I'll need a staff if I move into that house. Do you know how to go about that?"

"I do. I can help with all kinds of things if you'll let me." She said she'd work on that as well. "Then we'll get it taken care of together."

When he was in his office he made the necessary calls to have the house furnishings appraised. There was a lot of it, from what Grace had said, so he told his buddy, Mark Morris, to bring an assistant. Then Lincoln asked him about an auction.

"You came to the right guy on that. My father has decided that he'd like to start doing them and has hired a couple old timers to help with it. They're having more fun than working, but it eventually gets done. Last week he did a large estate and it took them all day, but there wasn't an unhappy person there. He said that he'd not felt this young in ages. I think he's right. And Mom is glad to have him out of the house more." They laughed. "But seriously, if she's willing to put up with people going around to look at things, then we'll have it right there. Could save her some bucks and headache."

"She's all for having less worry right now. Ginger—her name is Ginger Rice—inherited the Conrad estate." Mark whistled. "Yes, it's a lot bigger than we knew, but then I thought it all belonged to Walton senior. Come to find out, she owned it all."

"How did she inherit? I thought they had this ass of a son." He told him what he knew of the situation, and Mark said he was sorry to hear that. "I mean, I never cared for either Walton, but she seemed nice. Well, quiet, but very nice when I had to talk to her about something."

Mark arranged to stay a few days with him and Grace, and to look over the household with his dad. They were very close and when he said that they'd make a week of it, Lincoln was thrilled. To have someone around for a few days would keep him out of trouble. He'd been banned from the studio just last night.

He supposed that she had a right to stop him from going there again. He had scared her, then his attempt to get her naked had failed too. She was in the middle of painting and had it in her hair and all over her hands, and he thought it sexy. Grace, however, hadn't. When she cried, he didn't know what to do and held her. That only worked for a few minutes.

"The muse is driving me insane." He asked her what he could do. "I'm not sure you can do anything. He wants — whoever this is, me to finish his story on canvas, and he doesn't care that I'm exhausted."

"Was it like that with the others?" She shook her head, her tears making him ache for her. "I wish I could tell you that I'll have a talk with him, but I don't even know how to do that. Come in the house and take a nap."

"I'm not seven." He moved back from the heat of her temper. "Look, I have to finish this or he's never going to let me go. I don't like this man, and couldn't care less for his story, but whatever he wants, I have to do."

"You're being silly." As soon as the words left his mouth, he knew that it had been the wrong thing to say. Not only did her temper go off the charts, but she turned away and told him to get out. "Honey, I'm so sorry."

"Just leave me alone, Lincoln, so I can get this finished."

He'd left her then, but he'd not been happy about it. And

while he was sitting in his office, in the dark, he decided to look up things like this. It said she was being silly as well. But he didn't tell her that when she came in at midnight to go to sleep.

He decided to talk to her now. Lincoln thought about groveling and would if that's what it took. He couldn't stand to have this trouble between them, especially since he was the one that had done it. Knocking on the door, he entered when she yelled for him to go away. As soon as he saw her, he could tell something else had happened.

"What is it? What's wrong, baby? Is Walton here?" She kissed him, and he held her to his body. "I like that, but why did you look so worried?"

"I had a long talk with myself. Muse too, I guess." He asked her how that had gone. "Well, I think. He's going to back off a bit, I believe because I have the first of the series done. Would you like to see it?"

"Yes. If you don't mind. You've been so hush-hush with this one." She took him to the area where she had put the others ready to be picked up any day now by Garrett. "You've made use of this entire building already. Do we need to expand your space?"

"I need someone to work the stretcher for me. Or buy the larger canvas for these projects." He said that would be easy. "I hope. Building them, starting from scratch, is good for the smaller paintings, but the big ones, such as this, is too hard on me. And then I have to call the faeries to help me move them into the other room where the lighting is better."

"It is?" He didn't think that was possible, as every rafter had a light on it. "Did you get help with that? I'm not good with you climbing on ladders to hang stuff up."

"The faeries and brownies did it. They were so thrilled that I hope you don't mind, but I had Mildred bring out some sugar cubes and her leftover flowers for them. They really like those, don't they?"

"They do. It's sort of like crack for them. They can get really high if they eat too much." She nodded and turned on the light to the other part of the barn. "Oh honey, this is more beautiful than the other."

"They helped me lift it up to this wall." He nodded as he took in the entire scene. "It's the wolf clan, the Canon wolves."

The painting was of the pack, perhaps a dozen or so, all gray and whites that seemed as if they'd just come from a killing. Their muzzles were covered in blood, and there was almost an air of excitement to them all. The bigger wolf, he'd bet it was Hank, was looking right at him like he was there and not just a painting.

"This is Hank's father. He looks so much like him, doesn't he? He is the one that is telling me the story. He's worried that his son is bored being the alpha and wanted me to show him how they looked when they were all around." Lincoln asked why he'd be bored. "I don't know, but his dad died only a few years ago, and he's saddened that he had to leave him so soon."

"He was ancient. I don't know how old, but I know that Hank is hundreds of years himself." She said that she knew that. "And this painting, will there be more to it?"

"Yes, I have two more done. Would you like to see them?" He did and went with her to the canvases. The first was of a man and little boy fishing. He knew it was Hank when he was younger. He remembered him like this. The older man was his father, Grace told him. They were sitting on a beach near a lake and enjoying the evening. "His name was Hank as well, but no one called him that. He was always called Sire, I guess because he was the first. But he wanted his son to remember the good times that they had too, not just the violence of life that they've all led. The second is in winter. They're playing as wolves in the snow."

It was beautiful. There were fluffs of snow coming down that looked real. And the two wolves were having a good time, like children left on their own. In the background, under a great oak, sat Sire as he watched the children before him.

"This is the pack meeting area. Sire picked it after this day to always remember that there was goodness coming from their lands. He loved that all of his children were around him when there weren't meetings too." He looked at the other figure, the one hidden almost out of sight from the wolves playing. "It's a human there, isn't it?"

"No. I mean yes. It's Coop, your father, as he might have been as a human. His face isn't there because he couldn't think how he'd look. And he didn't want him to look too much like Cooper. But he knew that the dragons watched over them as much if not more than he did them. It's why they are always so willing to help us—they have been a part of this group since the beginning."

The paintings were incredible, and he couldn't stop staring at them. Grace told him that there would be four more, all of them a memory that he had with his family. When he asked if she was going to sell them, Grace told him that Sire had begged her to, and to not let his son buy any of them.

"But I asked if he could have a picture of them, for himself. And he consented to that. I really do speak to them, Lincoln. I want you to know I'm not being silly."

"I know that, love. And I'm profoundly sorry for what I said. I hope you can forgive me." She laid her head on his chest and he felt better already. "Can I come in and chase you around the tables again?"

"Yes, right now would be wonderful." She backed from him and began taking off her shirt. "I've been so busy that I forgot how much I enjoy when you make love to me. How I feel like I'm on top of the world when you do."

He started to pull off his own clothing when she smiled at him. It was a wonderful feeling, how much he loved her. And her smiling at him like he was king of the world.

~~~

Grace wanted to touch Lincoln. Not just to make love, but to feel his skin against hers, to have his breath mingle with her own. And when he caressed her, his fingers brought on so many emotions, it felt like her heart was too full for all the love she felt for him.

"I love the way your skin feels when I touch it."

She moaned when he nipped at her throat. Taking off her bra, he stood behind her and ran his fingers up and down her spine. It made her feel taller, her body stronger to have him touching her like this. When he cupped her, Grace felt her nipples harden and her breasts swell with need. But he only teased her.

Her pants were simple leggings. She found them easier to move around in rather than a pair of jeans or jogging pants. They were skin tight on her, and she thought that they were easier on her legs too. As he pulled them off her, taking her panties with them, Lincoln kissed every inch of her flesh as he exposed her to him.

"Have you any idea how much I love looking at your body? If I were a painter, I'd only paint you in the nude. I love the way your muscles look when you're aroused. The way your nipples pink up in anticipation of me taking them into my mouth." Moaning again, he ran his fingers over the tops of her breasts to her nipples and they tightened more. "Your skin is soft yet so very strong. I could hold you like this all day."

"Please? I need to touch you too." He told her not yet, it was his turn. "We're taking turns? The next time I have you in bed, I'm going to use mine to make you suffer in ways you can't imagine."

"Oh, but I can imagine a great deal. Like you bent over that table and me fucking you from behind. I can imagine you standing against the wall, my cock buried so deep inside of you that you don't know if it's me or you that you can feel there. I will be a part of you, we'll be one." His words were like flames over her body. "Come on, my love. Lean over there for me and let me have my way."

She moved to the large table, and was thankful it was screwed to the floor. Otherwise she was sure that they'd move it across the room before they were finished. When he came up behind her, his cock between her legs, she felt her pussy juices, and the thickness of his cock being soaked with it. At his moan she laid her head down on the table and waited for him to take her. In fact, all she could think about was having this man inside her.

His hands moved up and down her back, his thumbs at her spine rubbing hard enough that she moaned for the pure pleasure of it. And as he massaged her, making her muscles pliable, softer, she was getting wetter and wetter with each stroke.

"I need you." He growled low as he nipped at her ribs this time, his cock moving over her pussy until she thought she'd die from the pleasure of it. "Lincoln, fill me, please. I need you to take me."

He did, but gently so. Like he was doing just as she wished, filling her with himself. As he made love to her body this way, holding her breasts from beneath, telling her how much he loved her with not just his mouth but his hands as well, Grace fell in love with him again. Her heart was so full for him that it was overflowing into the rest of her body. So that when he cupped her, sliding his fingers into her pussy with his cock, Grace came apart, screaming out his name over and over until he bit her.

His teeth were longer than his human ones. As he sank them into her flesh, she came again and again. It was like she was being impaled by him, marked in some way, and when he came with her, giving her more than she'd ever dreamed of getting from any person, her body stiffened once more as she screamed for him to finish her, and he touched his finger to her clit, bringing her such relief that she fainted from it.

When she woke she was lying on the cot with Lincoln spooned behind her. She knew that he was awake — his fingers were dancing up and down her arm. It was as if he couldn't get enough of her. The same way she felt about him.

"Your show is in three days. I'd almost forgotten about

it." She turned and looked at him. "The family is going, I think you might have known that, but I wanted to tell you some of the faeries are going to keep an eye on things for you." She rolled to her back and he looked down at her. "When is Garrett coming to get these paintings?"

"In the morning. He said that he has it all set up the way he wants it to look. He just needs to get them in place. And some of my other paintings will be there as well. I found a few when my art supplies were brought from the house I was staying at before you barged into my life. Thank you for that." He kissed her. "I'm not as nervous this time. I know that I can sell or not, and it's not going to break me."

"Are you going to let Hank see these?" She told him she wasn't sure. "I think you should, but that's just me. And if he wants to buy them, tell him what you told me about his father."

"Will he believe me?" Lincoln told her that he'd believe her more than anyone would. He was a spirit animal. "I don't know what that means."

"His image is on a totem pole. Something that they hold very special in their hearts. And not only that, when one of them passes from this life to the next, they believe that they're born into the body of the next child. It's the beliefs that they've had since they were made." She thought about the next painting in the series. "What are you thinking, love? That you don't believe their story?"

"No, nothing like that. I was thinking of the next painting. It's of a totem pole, but not like the ones you see now. I mean, they have them in Indian camps and such on television. This is made of stone. Carved into the long piece of granite by someone much stronger than anyone in their pack. The carvings are of an eagle, who is perched at the top. Then the wolf, a bear, then the face of a woman. She's so beautiful that it defies words. Her name is Dawn, mother of all earth."

"Mother of all faeries is Dawn. Is it her?" She said she'd never met her, but that sounded about right. "When you show this to Hank, ask him what they mean. I'm sure if anyone knows, it's going to be him."

"I'll call him now." They both got up to dress, excitement racing over her skin. "The image is all drawn in, but not painted yet. I can tell him what it's going to look like before I can give him the pictures Sire said he can have."

"Why is that, I wonder?" She knew, but wasn't to tell anyone. Not until Hank said the words aloud. "I'll make the call now if you want to get them ready. He might be able to come right away."

After he got off the phone with the alpha, she stood in front of the canvas where she'd penciled in the drawing. She hadn't had to do that to the other and didn't understand why until now.

Hank would be seeing it today, and she wasn't going to start painting until tomorrow. Sire wanted him to know that he was thinking of something important that only Hank knew about and could take care of. And whatever it was, he wanted her to tell the story. And when the alpha got there, she was to tell him that he must do it soon. For whatever reason, something was about to happen, and Sire wanted it taken care of.

As soon as the alpha showed up, she had a feeling that he wished to be anywhere but here. Something had happened, and when he told them about the contractor buying up the land on the other side of their mountain, she knew. The totem was there, and it could be damaged or found when they started working. Showing him the painting had more importance now, and she was glad that she could help him.

"That is the pole of my people. It was carved by a great dragon, a witch, and a sorcerer." Lincoln asked where it was. Laughing, he told them. "It's in the mountain. A path that leads to it is said to have been there since the beginning of time. We have our greatest events there. Weddings, the announcement of a newborn. Also, the death of one of our kind. I've not thought of it in many years. My father, I think, was the last to have used it."

"Why do you think he wanted you to know about it now?" Hank looked at her. "I'm sorry. But he didn't tell me anything other than to show you this painting."

"If the men blast, as I think they're going to, the totem of life will be harmed. I don't know this for sure, but even if a part of it is broken off, then all our magic will as well. It's our power, our life—it's why we use it, or did, for such events. I'll have it moved right away." She asked how he was to do that. "The earth. I will ask, and if she's of a mind to, which I think she will be, then she'll help me move it. It's her face there, the one that has started this all for us."

"Your father, he said that you couldn't buy any of the paintings. Do you know why?" Hank laughed, which brought a smile to her face. "You know, don't you?"

"He never liked what he called foo-foo things. There are few in the pack house. A picture of him. A horn that was on a great animal from long ago, and a few daggers that were a part of the first tools that we used. Yes, he'd say that. It would be clutter to him, foo-foo or unnecessary items. But I would, if you could, like pictures of them. Especially the one of the two wolves playing in the snow." She told him that she'd make sure he got a good one too. "Thank you, my friend. You may have saved us a great many heartaches with your news. If you should need anything, let me know and I'll have it for you."

"Thank you. And your father, he wanted me to give you a message. He said that your son needs to go to college — that you should send him." Hank laughed again. "He also said that you can laugh at him should you want, but you know him to be telling you the truth."

"I do. And thank you again."

He left with the pack that had come with him. When they were gone, she leaned into Lincoln, who stood behind her, and closed her eyes. Peace rolled over her. And the muse thanked her for her help.

Chapter 10

Walton moved to stand in the shadow of the barn. He knew that she was here, and the sooner he got her, the faster he could get out of town. He wasn't sure how that was to work yet, but once he had his little boy he'd be home free. Things would finally start to go his way. He saw her before she turned and was glad that he'd been here to see it. Ginger was there, and she was holding his son like she was somebody.

"I know you're there." He turned to look, but it could only have been him that she was talking to. "You've been stalking me for three days, and it's time we finished this. I'm going to tell you now, you'd be better off running. But knowing you, instead of running from the trouble you're causing, you'll head right to it."

"I want him. You give me little Walton and I'll go away without hurting you. I know you're here all alone—stupid as usual on your part—but I want my son." She told him she wasn't going to give him up. "You will when I kill you."

147

"Will you? I don't think so. And besides, you have always thought me stupid, and yet here I am, the person that your poor dear mother left everything to." That shocked him, and he told her that she lied. "I'm not. Don't you read the papers? I'm an heiress. People are lining up to tell me how glad they are that you didn't get the money. There was quite a bit of it too, Walton. More than enough to take care of her grandson."

"You'll have to sign that over to me, Ginger. It's my son and money. My mother wasn't anything but a stupid cow who murdered my father. You don't deserve it any more than she did." She told him it was hers in the first place. "Yes, yes, I heard that too. But Father had to take it from her because she was so bad with it. All women only want to go shopping, and I would imagine that my mother was no different. He saved her from being poor."

"You think that, do you? From what I've been made to understand, she ran a multimillion-dollar company while under his rule, and when he told her that she was to sign over her holdings to him, she didn't. Your mother was brave in that. He might well have lost it like he did most of the holdings he had before they were married." Again, he called her a liar and asked why she'd say such thing. "It's the truth, whether you want to believe it or not."

"It doesn't matter who had what. It should have come to me, and I want it. I'll need it to raise my son." She told him no and laid the little bundle at her feet. "What are you going to do now? Fight me? Good. Come on, Ginger. It'll be like old times. I'll knock you around until you're out cold, then I'll take my son and we'll all be happy."

"You're not taking him. I've decided that I don't want you

around either. I'm not going to be looking over my shoulder at every dark shadow that might be you."

He laughed, not sure where all this bravado was coming from, but he'd surely knock that out of her soon enough. Taking a step toward her, he was surprised when she didn't back away. It was a game that they had played all the time when she'd been with him. It made the chase more fun when she was afraid of him.

"What's gotten into you? You used to know the rules of the game. You need to play with me or it'll not go well for you. Come on now, I'll hit you and you're going to cower on the ground." She said that she wasn't afraid of him any longer. "You'd better be. I'm going to knock the shit out of you and take my son. Then you're going to be a good girl and give me what I want."

"I'm never giving anyone what they want again. You're nothing to me." He lunged toward her and she moved. It was fast, like she was prepared for anything that he put out. Well, he wasn't having it. Not today. When she was far enough away from the baby, he snatched him up. Looking down at it, he saw that it was nothing more than a kid's doll. A girl at that.

"What the fuck is this?" She laughed, and he had a moment of fear. It didn't sound at all like Ginger. "What are you doing with my kid, Ginger?"

"Not Ginger." While he watched she changed from his wife to something else. The creature standing before him looked like a giant bug, one that had wings and sparkled when they moved. "I'm Winnie. Someone that you should fear, but I know you won't. You are stupid, aren't you?"

"Where's my son? Where is Ginger? Tell her that I want her to bring him here, and my money. It's mine, you fucking cunt!" She asked why he had to resort to name calling. "You called me stupid."

"No, I said that you were, I didn't call you that. And I'm not going to get her here, you won't get that precious little boy, and you are never going to terrorize anyone again." She laughed, and he felt that same shiver of fear run over him. "You really should pay attention to your surroundings, Stupid. And yes, that time I did call you Stupid."

He turned around when she nodded to his left. And when he did, Walton quickly turned back to stare at the woman, or whatever the fuck she was. But when she walked by him, taking the little dolly with her, he turned too. There were five of the biggest fucking dragons that he'd ever seen — of course, he'd only seen one before, but they were fucking huge. The man with them came toward him, and he knew it was one of the Mannings. It occurred to him that all the rumors were true. They were dragons.

"Hello, Walton. I've been waiting for you to come here. It's a shame that you had to make it today — we're sort of pressed for time." He said he'd come back. "No, no. I'd rather get this over with, wouldn't you?"

"What do you think you're going to do? Kill me? Not going to happen. I don't know how you're making those dragons, but you won't let them hurt me, will you?" The man just nodded, and one of them blew a stream of fire so close to his feet that he jumped back from it. "What the fuck is wrong with you? You could have killed me."

"That's the plan, you see. We're going to make sure that

you're dead before we go to the gallery tonight." He asked where Ginger was. "Oh, she's feeding Wendall. And then she and her sister are going to get dressed for the opening tonight. It's really too bad that you can't be there. Well, it's not—you weren't invited anyway. But you're going to die today, and that'll be the end to all your terror."

"Just like that? You think you're going to kill me like I'm nothing at all. People know that I'm here." He said that they didn't, nor did anyone care. "They do. I've got plenty of friends that'll avenge my death."

"Doubtful. You have no friends, and the crew that you hung out with are all in prison, where you should be." He said that he'd been released. "No, you escaped, and that's a big difference. And the police have said that we might handle this in any way that we wish. Nice of them, don't you think?"

"I want to go back to jail." The dragons took a step toward him and he felt the ground rumble with their weight. "I don't want you to kill me like this. I have no idea how you think you're going to manage this, but you can't do it."

"Oh, but we can." The dragons were standing around him, each a different hue of blue. He might have thought it was pretty but for the fact that he was about to piss his pants. "Walton Conrad, the last of your family, the worse man that I've ever had the displeasure of meeting. I hereby sentence you to death by fire—the only way that my family can be safe, the only way to rid this world of your reign."

The first flame of fire touched his face. It wasn't so bad, but he felt the heat of it on the rest of his body before he could laugh in their faces. Then they all sprayed their heat at him, and it was then that he realized he was going to die. When

151

they suddenly stopped, he lay on the ground; there wasn't a part of his body that didn't hurt. And when Ginger or her sister, he could no longer tell, came to stand in front of him, she threw cash at him.

"This is all you wanted. Blood money." He tried his best to grab it all up before she laughed at him again. "Even with your own death staring you in the face, you cannot let a little of the money you fought so hard to steal get away, can you?"

"Son," he said as best he could, and she only shook her head. "Want. Son." His lips no longer worked. He couldn't even lift his hands to see what was the matter with them. He was going to die, and he wasn't sure right now that he cared. He hurt that badly. "Son."

"You have no son. He will never know of you. For as long as I live, I will never tell him that you were his father. He'll never be like you. Never be the man that you are. He'll be good and kind. He'll be my son, and I'll raise him the way I want."

The flames hit him again; this time he was sure they were making him suffer. The pain was incredible. He hurt so badly that he wasn't sure there was anywhere they'd missed. As he lay there, his body on fire, he thought of his son and wondered if he'd remember him despite his mother. No, no one would remember him at all.

Closing his eyes, or attempting to, he could still see the dragons. They were finished, he thought — no more fire came his way. As the biggest came forward, he prayed for help, but was sure that the only help he was going to get was death. Walton didn't think anyone could come back from this much fire.

The shadow of the dragon's foot covered him. In that last moment of his life, Walton thought of his son, and wondered once again if he'd remember him fondly. Then nothing.

~~~

Grace went to find her sister after the body was taken care of. What she had done, said to the man, was the bravest thing she'd ever seen. She'd stood up to her tormentor and then walked away. But Grace knew what it had cost her, and when she found her on the back deck, she didn't say anything but sat down beside her.

"What do you suppose my son will say when he finds out that I had his father killed?" Grace was trying to think of an answer when Ginger continued. "Not only did I watch him be killed, but I denied him his dying wish."

"Do you think he would have done the same for you had you been dying by his hand? You think he would have shown you any mercy at all when he murdered you and Mattie?" Ginger said that he'd have not hurt her. "Yes, he would have. She was in his way. He would have taken her, used her to get you to bring him Wendall, then he would have killed you both. He hurt her before."

"But I stood by while he suffered." This time she didn't answer her. "He killed a lot of people, just to get to me. And he would have done more too, wouldn't he?"

"Yes. He was determined to get his little boy, as he called him. And to get back at you. I'm serious when I tell you that he would have taken Mattie and killed you both." Ginger laid her head on her shoulder, just like when they were kids. "I'm glad that you got to have closure with this. And to know that he'll never bother you again. I'm so proud of you, Ginger."

153

"I'm proud of you as well. My little sister is making a name for herself." Grace pointed out that she was only twenty minutes older than her. "Yes, well, having two kids and a maniac chaining me to a bed, making me service him all the time, makes me considerably older than those lousy minutes."

They were both laughing when the men and women joined them. Winnie commented on how even she was proud of Ginger, and that she'd done a very good job of making sure he knew who was boss. Carson said that she might not have been able to do something like that and was jealous of her bravery. All in all, Grace realized that having support like this was the best thing to have.

Ginger went in to feed Wendall and Grace headed out to the studio. Yesterday the men had finished putting in the insulation for her to have warmth in the winter months, and the air conditioner and furnace were done as well. Going into the drying room, as she'd begun to call it, she looked around at the empty area. The paintings had been picked up last night.

Someone was coming in today to make her several large canvases. And she was excited about getting a start on the next series. The muse was being quiet for a change, so Grace painted what she wanted, and that was her sister and her two children. It was fun for her to be able to make this gift for her, and she wanted it to be perfect. By the time Lincoln joined her, she had them marked and ready for detail to be put in.

"There was a phone call for you. Ginger took it. It was your parents." She turned and looked at him, the painting forgotten. "They just read about your sister being a new mom and seemed to have not known about Mattie. How is that possible?"

"They are usually too into whatever they're doing to realize that they have children. Ginger and I left home when we were sixteen. We've not been back to see them since. So, it's been twelve years." He asked what they were doing. "Whatever shiny thing that came along. They weren't good to us, thinking that since we were no longer requiring them to feed us or change our diapers, then we were old enough to fend for ourselves. So, we did. It's small wonder that they even took the time to call."

"That does not sound like a loving grandparent, or even parent for that matter." She said they weren't and put her brushes away. "I've ruined your mood. I'm so sorry."

"No, I am sorry. I don't want them to come here. And I'm betting that Ginger doesn't either. I'd expect them sometime, but they'll neither stay long nor will they be very proud of either of us. Not my accomplishments, nor the fact that Ginger has money." Lincoln asked if they'd try to take money from them. "Oh no, that's not their style. They won't even ask, even if they thought that they could convince us to give it to them. They just don't care about anything we do or what we might have that they don't. They're cold, heartless people."

"Wow, I'm truly sorry." She smiled at him. "That doesn't look like a friendly smile, love. What are you planning in that head of yours? Trouble?"

"No, but I'm betting that Ginger wishes she'd not taken the call for me." He laughed. "Garrett wants me to be at the gallery at five for a preview of what he's done. I told him that I trusted him and he's happy with that, but wants me to come in. He's also told me that he wants the wolf paintings too."

"I've got a photographer coming in the morning. Are they

dry enough to move? I think he wants to take them outside for better lighting." She said that they'd be all right. "And I have the drywaller coming tomorrow as well. They'll hang the last of it while we're in town if that's okay with you."

"Yes. I'll make sure that everything is covered so that no dust gets onto anything. And thank you for the garage door. It'll make getting some of the smells that linger out of here faster. Not to mention I'll be able to move my work to the doorway when it's not too cold out to paint by natural sunlight." He bowed to her. "Have I told you lately that I love you? I do. Very much so."

"And I love you. Very much so." He hugged her, and she wrapped her arms around his waist and let him hold her. "So, we're done talking about your parents?"

"Yes. They aren't in our lives anymore, and that's the way we'll keep it. If Ginger doesn't get talked into inviting them here." He asked if she would. "I don't know. She's still on a pretty good high about Walton being gone. Not that he's dead, but the freedom of not having to worry about him any longer."

"All right then. We'll deal with it if we have to." She thanked him. "Mark is coming next week. He is excited to see the Conrad estate. If this works out for him and Ginger, he said that he'd travel to the other homes and deal with them as well. I don't know that he has any idea what sort of things are in this house in town, but you can bet he'll make her the best deal on it all."

"I thought they were going to have an auction." Lincoln said that Mark was going to buy some of the pieces himself and then have an auction. "That'll be good. She said that whatever she makes off this, she's going to set up a fund at the high school in Molly's name, the Molly Conrad Foundation. Whatever it is, I'm going to donate to it as well from the sale of my paintings."

"We will as a family too. Cooper has been talking about college funds for a couple weeks now. This will be a good one for us to start on." She moved to clean up her area and he sat down on the table. "Sadie is coming over when we get back. She's talked to Winnie—I guess they knew each other before she helped my dad. Winnie has convinced, or partially so, Cooper that she really has something of our dad's and wants to make sure that he gets it. I'm curious what it could be."

"I would be too. I mean, your father has been gone for a very long time, hasn't he?" Lincoln told her more years than they could count. "I hope whatever it is brings you all joy. To have something from someone that loved you that much would be amazing. Especially after all this time."

Ginger came out to talk to her about their parents, and Lincoln said that he had to go into town for some projects he had to get going. Grace asked her what they wanted now. And were they coming here.

"I didn't get that they wanted anything. They read about your showing and told me how they knew you had talent. I don't know how they would have, but I didn't say anything. And they are coming, but only for a day or two. They have other commitments." Ginger laughed. "They want to drive on out to the coast before it gets too terribly cold, then they're headed back home. I guess Dad finally got a job, and he worked until he retired and they're spending all his pension on travel. And I'm quoting her here, 'they only have a few years left to do all the things they want.' I asked about seeing the kids and they said if they have time — they've never really liked children."

"Good old Mom; never be tactful when being rude can do it so much faster. Did she hurt you with that?" Ginger said no, she had expected it. "I'm sorry."

"Don't be. I don't care if they come or not. If they do, then okay, we'll see them, and they'll move on. If not, what are we out? Nothing. They're the ones that did this to us, and I've no desire to see about patching things up with them now. I'm a bigger person, and a much better mom."

"You are at that. The best mom there is, as a matter of fact." They both laughed, and it felt good. "Did Lincoln tell you that Mark is coming next week? You'll be able to get rid of all that crap now. And I heard that the local used clothing store is taking all the clothes from the house for you."

"Yes, it's really nice how they're even going to come get them. Someone needs to be there. They prefer a police officer, just so we can't say they took something that didn't belong to them." Ginger snorted. "Whatever they wanted to take, I'd be glad to get rid of it. It's all going anyway."

They talked about nothing much while she gathered up her list of supplies that she needed ordered. She had applied for a sales license and gotten it. Now she was ordering in bulk, and it was really nice to have so much on hand that she didn't have to not finish a painting because she didn't have the right color or brush.

"I was thinking about this showing tonight." Grace asked if she was going. "I am. But I wanted to ask if you had a dress I could borrow. I want to look fabulous tonight. I have no idea, but you know how it is, you want to look pretty for yourself."

"Yes, you can borrow anything I have, you know that— and you are pretty. Beautiful even. And you are an amazing person. You don't treat yourself like you know that anymore." Ginger thanked her. "You're very welcome. And I think I have the perfect dress for you. When I was trying some on for this thing, the lady sent out a bunch of them for me to try on. I took the black one, and you can wear the white that looks just like it."

"You think that'll be all right? I mean, we're twins. Won't it be childish for us to wear matching clothes?" Grace told her that they were adults, and they could damn well do what they wanted. "You're right. I'm game if you are."

Going up to her room, Grace got the dresses and took them to Ginger. They were going to start getting ready for this thing anyway; they might as well make a girls' afternoon of it. She told Lincoln what they were doing. Not the dresses, but that they were getting ready.

Mark has made it early. He's going to the gallery with us. I hope you don't mind. She said that she didn't. *Good. Also, flowers arrived for you from your parents. I read the card because— well, I didn't know who would be sending my girl flowers. And I understand now about them.*

What did the card say? He read it to her. *Yes, well that's them in a nutshell. All right, we'll be ready in a couple hours. You will be completely blown away by how beautiful we are.*

I am every time you come into a room. And it doesn't matter what you have on either. I think you're the most gorgeous creature ever created. She told him she loved him. *You are my heart, Grace, and will be forever.*

Closing the connection, she told Ginger that Mom and Dad weren't going to come after all. Then she told her what the note said. They both got a good laugh over it.

"They actually said, 'We've thought it over and we don't want to see the children. They're very messy. Maybe next time we come through.'" Ginger shook her head. "Not even a love, just a simple Mom and Dad. They're so wonderful, aren't they? Not really."

Tonight, they were going to have a good time, despite their parents being assholes. Messy indeed. As they got dressed, she wondered about her sister and finding someone to love. She of all people deserved it.

Chapter 11

Lincoln couldn't believe his eyes. Ginger and Grace looked like bookends, and they were stunning together. Not that they weren't apart, but when they stood side by side like they were now, he couldn't think beyond the exquisiteness.

"Holy shit, Lincoln, please tell me that the one in white isn't seeing anyone." He glanced at Mark and asked why. "Because, my dear friend, she's my mate."

"No way." Mark nodded and looked like a man who had been given all his Christmas gifts early. "She's not, but has two children and has had a rough time lately."

Lincoln told him briefly as they posed for pictures what had happened. Mark listened and asked a few questions, like was the guy taken care of. After telling him about that, he told him that she was as fragile as a rose and could be just as thorny when pushed.

"I'll take care of her. And I will go easy too. I can't even imagine what she's gone through and come up on the other

side of it. That shows you how smart and brave she is."
Lincoln knew that he would too.

Mark wasn't a dragon but a tiger, like Garrett. That was
how he'd met him. He knew some about the other man, but
not enough to form an opinion one way or the other. Lincoln
decided to talk to Garrett when things settled down at tonight.

They took separate cars to the opening. It wasn't like
they'd fit in the limo anyway. So, as they were driving over,
he told Grace what Mark had said about Ginger.

"If he hurts her, what happened to Walton will be nothing
compared to what I do to him. I'll hire Winnie if I need to. I'm
to understand that she has some experience in making people
suffer." He looked at her then back at the road.

"You've become quite protective over the last few days."
Grace asked what he meant. "This morning I was holding
Wendall and you told me if I dropped him you'd do the same
to me from the top of the house. Then when we were in the
hallway, you tied my tie too tight and told me that you'd see
me hanged if I stepped out on you."

"That would be the muse. She's really aggressive in
getting what she wants." She laughed and told him she'd have
a talk with her. "I don't think she has had a good relationship
with men. But she does have an eye for art. We're working on
a scene now that is going to be epic. I am excited."

He had long since given up on trying to figure out why she
had this other person inside of her that spoke to her when she
was working. When she talked about them, it was as if they
were real, someone that she had to listen to or the painting
was all wrong. He'd been watching her one day, while she'd
been in the studio, and heard her talking with the muse or

whoever was guiding her. And it was the strangest thing he'd ever witnessed. It was like listening to a phone conversation and not knowing what was being said on the other end of the call.

The gallery was empty when they got there. Lincoln walked around with Grace to see how the paintings looked now that they were in this setting. The large painting was front and center, and he had an idea that there was going to be a great deal of talk about it when people arrived. The sold sign on it was small, but the price that had been paid was still visible. His brother had gotten a great piece.

"The newspaper is here. And two news vans. I didn't call them." Garrett was apologetic but excited too. "They'll bring you to the front of every art critic in the world, I bet. And they'll all love you after tonight." Grace squeezed tighter on his arm. "The photographer was here earlier, and took some snaps of all the smaller ones, but said he'd have to return to get the large one. He didn't have the right lens or something."

"He told me when he left. I didn't even know that you could change out the lens on a camera to make it wide. I don't have a lot to do with cameras unless you count my phone. And most of those pictures are of my niece and nephew." Garrett laughed, and Lincoln saw Mark speaking to Ginger.

Mark wasn't having an easy time of it. And after talking to Garrett about him, Lincoln wasn't worried about Ginger any longer. The man, apparently, had a heart of gold, and he had money. That had been something else that had worried Lincoln, someone coming along to take her for a ride. Garrett assured him that Ginger was Mark's mate—he could smell it on them.

"What does that mean?" Grace, in her muse mode again, asked Garrett, and he took a step back. Lincoln explained. "I'm sorry. I'm trying to keep her under control, but she wants me to paint. What do you mean, you can smell it on them? Please?"

"He touched her at some point. I don't mean sexually, though that scent would be stronger if they had. But once they did, skin to skin, they were both marked. Cats are very territorial, and he had to make sure that no one else poached on his woman." Grace cocked a brow at Garrett, who laughed. "You are adorable when you're all protective. But you don't have to worry about Mark. He's one of the best men I know, besides the Mannings."

"She's been through a great deal. Ginger doesn't need some dick trying to horn in on her life and take it over. She's just getting to the point where she's making decisions about her own life. If he takes that from her, I'm going to make him into a dickless wonder." Garrett told her that her muse was showing again. "No, that was all me. I love Ginger, and she's all the family that I want to have anything to do with besides Lincoln's. Mark better not fuck this up."

"No, I can assure you that he won't." Garrett said he had to check on some things and left them standing there. Lincoln took her into his arms and kissed her head.

"You're scaring the nice man, Grace." She looked at him with an impish smile. "Oh, I see. That was the goal. And what do you have planned now that we're semi alone?"

"We're going to help Mark." He asked her how they were going to do that. "We'll go talk to them and convince my sister that she is as good as married to the man. Just let me handle it."

"Will it be you, or the muse? I'm sort of worried about this one if you want the truth. You're all mean and murderous. I'd almost be afraid to see you if you were able to shift into something." She laughed and told him she was fine. And so was he. "And Mark? Will he be all right with you in your current mood?"

"I don't know. Why don't we go find out?"

Lincoln went with her, but he didn't let go of her arm. He was going to protect them both if he could. But this muse was very odd. He wondered what sort of paintings would come out of it. Laughing, all he could imagine was bondage and whips.

"Hello, you must be Mark. I've heard all about you." He shook her hand and congratulated her on the show. "I've been working toward this my whole life, I think. My sister has been my biggest supporter. I'm very protective of her."

"I have no intentions of hurting her." He looked at Ginger as he continued. "I was just telling her about myself and why I'm being such a pest. She said that Garrett explained about mates and things with a cat."

"I'm not sure this is a good thing." Lincoln asked Ginger why not. "I'm sort of sour on men, if you know what I mean. So far, I've had two children by two very abusive men. I can't handle anything more right now."

"I understand. I do. I'm not sure what has happened to you. Lincoln told me a little, but you must be very strong. You came out of those relationships a better person than I would have, I think." She asked Mark why he'd say that. "My parents were very abusive. Not the same thing, I know, but

165

they ended up killing my little brother with their abuse, and nearly did the same to me. I was lucky that someone came along and rescued me. Garrett's family took me in when my parents were killed by the leap for what they did."

"I'm so sorry. That must have been horrific as a child." He told Ginger that it had been worse losing his little brother. "I don't know what I'd do without Grace. She's been my rock for so long that I couldn't stand the thought of losing her."

"Yes, I understand that as well."

Lincoln thought they were getting closer and pulled Grace away to talk to her. She was all right with them, it seemed to him, so it wasn't really any kind of effort to get her to come with him.

"They're starting to line up. The newspaper is already here and wants to know if they can interview you." She looked at Lincoln when Garrett asked. "He can come along too. I love that you hold onto him when you think you're in over your head. You're not, Grace. You deserve this. You're that talented."

"He's always saying things like that to me. When inside I'm a bubbling mess of stomach acid that is about to erupt all over the nice clean floor." Lincoln laughed, and when she did as well, he knew she was feeling better. "I'm okay now. I just get antsy at the beginning."

"I'm not going to leave your side tonight. You just go with the flow, and when you're ready to take a break, I'll find us a nice dark corner and we'll neck a little." The first of the guests came through the hallway where they were standing. Cooper and Carson were behind them, and he could see Xavier there as well. "Any one of them will be your crutch should you need one."

"I know that. I think I have from the very start." He nodded and glanced into the room they'd left Ginger and Mark in. They were both gone, and he was happy for that. The two were perfect for each other.

As questions about the paintings came her way, Grace answered them with wit and charm. Lincoln wasn't positive, but he was sure that a couple of the older men had fallen in love with his mate. The more they walked around, talking about the paintings and her inspiration, the more relaxed Grace became. He was with her when someone asked where her models for the paintings had come from.

"My husband and I live on a lot of acreage, and the wolves are all around us. I see them occasionally, and that was enough for me to paint them." He asked if they were shifters. "I'm not sure what you mean; they're just wolves in a field."

The man was looking at the one where the two cubs were playing in the snow. He was very close to it, and she asked him to not touch. When he put out his finger, as if he was going to do so despite what she'd said, the man was suddenly on the floor screaming about the pain.

Garrett escorted him out after telling him that the next time he darkened his doorway, he was going to call the police. And for this man, Davie something, not to be surprised if they showed up to tell him there was a restraining order out on him. The rest of the showing went very well.

The guests were leaving around midnight. It was a long showing, even for the number of guests that had shown up. Garrett found them in the room with her other paintings, the ones that had nothing to do with the wolves, to tell her how the night went. He also had a man with him that he wanted to talk to Grace about.

"This is William Tennyson. He owns and operates Tennyson Gallery in New York." They all shook hands, and then Garrett looked at Grace as he continued. "He wants to represent you there. Bring your paintings to his gallery, and you'd be his primary artist. For an entire month."

"What about you?" Garrett told her that she'd outgrown his little gallery. "I don't understand. You don't want to have my paintings here anymore?"

"Oh yes, I'd love to have everything you have. But this man, he can make you a star. I can't do that. Not with the people that come through here." She looked at Lincoln, then back at Garrett. "He wants to help you become world famous. You deserve that."

"How many paintings did I sell tonight?" Garrett didn't even have to look. He told her all but one. "Okay, so you sold ninety-nine percent of my work. How would he do any better? Sell the last one? I thank you for your consideration, Mr. Tennyson, but for now, at least, I'm happy in this little gallery."

Then she simply walked away. Garrett looked so relieved that he wanted to hug him, and he felt like she'd made the right decision. When he caught up with her, she was leaning against the wall, wide eyed.

"I sold all but one? Did you hear him say that? One of those smaller paintings was marked at forty grand. And that was the lowest price that I could see." Lincoln told her congratulations. "No, you don't understand. I sold all but one. Could he be playing a trick on me? You know, saying that in front of the other man? That's it, isn't it? I'm going to find out."

They walked around the gallery twice, and Garrett had told the truth. If his calculations were right, she'd made just over two million dollars plus the painting that Cooper bought from her. And there wasn't one that didn't have a sticker on it. All of them had sold after all.

Lincoln was glad now that they'd gotten a hotel. There was no way he was going to be able to drive and comfort Grace. She was a basketcase.

~~~

Grace was sitting in the chair by the window when Lincoln joined her in the living room. She'd been there for a few hours, just letting the night before settle in. When he asked if she was all right, she nodded and looked outside.

"I had a call this morning from Ginger. She told me that Mark and she are getting along great, and that he wants to meet the kids." Lincoln asked if she was okay with that. "Oh yes. I like Mark, he seems nice. If he's not lying to her about things."

"He can't." She looked at Lincoln. "As mates, we can't lie to each other. Not even a white lie. And tigers are the worst at it. They're known to not even keep a secret from their mates. Makes Christmas buying a nightmare."

"Really? So, you can't to me either." He told her that he couldn't, but he wouldn't anyway. "Okay, then last night when I told that other man I didn't want to go use his gallery, did you think I was insane?"

"Never that. And I thought you did very well." She said that he'd not answered her. "I'm sorry, no, I don't think you

169

were. For a great many reasons. First, we've not done any kind of research on him. He could be minutes from bankruptcy, and we'd not know it until he took your paintings, and then the bank would take them for back taxes or something. Has he had any kinds of theft in the building? I would have asked that one straight away. No, darling, I think you were very smart in not jumping in with both feet. If you want to later, then we'll have him investigated."

"Did you have me investigated?" He nodded. "Why? When I got here, you didn't know I was your mate, did you? I mean, it's a smell thing."

"It is, and yes, you as well as your sister, because we were taking you into our home. And you might want to warn Ginger your parents are broke. As in they'll make it home, but there aren't going to be any more trips for them." She waved him off, knowing that was what they did. "But yes, we have everyone that we don't know personally investigated. Even Garrett, when you decided to use him as your gallery."

"I'm glad you did that for me. I wouldn't have even thought of that. I guess I'm too trusting." He told her that he'd been around a long time. "I suppose. Okay, so what else have you done for me behind the scenes, so to speak? And is Garrett doing all right?"

"Let me see. You're getting all your inventory for wholesale thanks to some favors that I pulled in. Nothing huge, but it does help when you make the prices for your work. I've put all the money that you're making into a safety deposit box. That way we don't hurt ourselves by putting it in the bank. We'll decide what to do with it when you're established." She liked that idea as well. "Garrett. Yes, he's doing all right, but with the two shows that you had there, he's finally out of the red for the year. Had you pulled and gone with Tennyson, he would more than likely have closed his doors. Which is a shame; he's got a lovely place and has room for expansion should he want."

"I want him to and I have an idea about that." He asked what it was. "I want to see about getting other artists in when I have a showing. Two or three should be enough. That way, I can draw them in and they can get their work out there. It's sort of what you did when you called Garrett for me."

"I love that idea. And, not to say you will bring in hordes of people, but you do bring in a buying crowd." She nodded, warming to the idea more and more. "Do you happen to know any fresh artists?"

"No, but I'm sure we can find them." He leaned back in the chair he was sitting in. "I want to go home soon too. I love our house, and I want to think about decorating some. Like the living room, to me, is perfect, but the rest of the house is a little on the bland side, don't you think?"

"I didn't want to waste time on getting them set up only to have you come in and change it all. Not you, but a mate of any kind. But yes, you're right, it does need something more done to it, and I love the living room too. Earth tones are my favorite, and I love how it makes us feel when we're in the room." He asked her about children.

"I would love to have some. I know that you and I can't have any, but we can adopt. I'm not sure how that works. But I think that having a home and savings account that isn't too shabby will help."

"Yes, it will. I just got a call from Hank. He has a child

that has lost his parents. All three were in a car accident about a week ago. Bradley, that's his name, was injured too, but they've set his leg and he'll be fine now. He's human, for the most part. His mother was entirely, his father half. That happens sometimes." She asked if they were going to take him. "If you want. I never told Hank anything either way. But the pack can't because of him being a human. It's against the pack laws."

"When can we adopt him? Today?" He asked if she'd marry him today. "Yes, I will. Everyone already thinks you're my husband; we might as well make it legal." He laughed, and she smiled.

"You're so romantic. How is your muse handling all this non-painting time? She all right with it?" She told him she supposed so. "Good. Then in the morning we'll get married at the courthouse, go home, and take our son there too. I'll have Drizzle find someone to buy us a few of the things we might need to bring him home. I don't suppose your sister could make us a list?"

"I'll ask her. And we really are getting married tomorrow?" He said yes and went to her on his knees. "What are you doing? Get up. I already said yes."

"You have, but what sort of husband would I be if I didn't get my new bride an engagement ring and wedding band? I had these made when we were here for your last showing. I haven't any idea why, but I thought you'd enjoy simple rather than flashy." She looked at the ring he put on her finger and thought it beautiful. A plain wide band with a single diamond in the middle. It was big, but still perfect. She kissed him for having it made for her. "You're very welcome, and tomorrow when we get home, we'll be a real family."

"As far as I'm concerned, we already are." A little boy. She was going to have a son to grow up with her nephew. "I do love you, Lincoln. I want you to always believe me when I say it."

"And I love you, Grace. And will for the rest of my days."

Lifting her up, he took her to the bed. She was still in her nightgown, and he made short work of that before joining her. Making love to this man was always wonderful. Even when he was in a hurry like when they were in her studio and he came out to harass her.

The kiss was gentle, and she moaned. His fingers were strong, and when he dug them into her tight muscles, it wasn't painful but felt good. Every part he touched, with either his mouth or fingers, soothed her. Her body was limp by the time he entered her and filled her like no other had before. She loved this man so much, she was sure that she'd never be able to tell him in words, but through making love.

When he lifted her up to meet his downward strokes, Grace cried out. Not in pain, but with pleasure. Her release was building, and the way he was taking her, it would be no time before she caught the one that would take her to the stars. It occurred to her that he never took his own pleasure until she had hers, several times as a matter of fact.

"Come love, so that I might show you the world." Nodding, her back bowed off the bed, her lungs filled to scream, and when he took her nipple into his mouth and bit down, Grace was sure that her body had come apart with the climax and flown away. "Again. Come for me once more."

Even though she told him no, she didn't have it in her,

Grace could feel it building. It wasn't gentle either, but her body seemed to be seized with the need to come. Holding onto him, knowing that she really was going to fly away, he cried out and brought her with him when he emptied into her.

Lincoln dropped on top of her and she didn't mind. He was heavy, but it was a good kind of weight. Holding him like she was, when he finally rolled to his back, she went with him and closed her eyes. She heard his soft snores even as she felt herself drifting off too.

Chapter 12

Cooper didn't think this was such a good idea. He had listened to all their arguments about why he should allow her to come talk to him, but he was still a little nervous. No longer angry at her, but he didn't think anything she had to tell him or give him would make a difference. It wasn't as if she was going to be able to bring his parents back.

When he'd seen her the other day, it hadn't brought up the memories that it did this time. As she came into the house, he remembered her from when he'd been a younger dragon. His father had gone to her for salves for cuts they'd receive. There were times when Dad would have taken her something he'd found while they were out foraging.

Cooper would never forget the day that his dad had died. Nor what it felt like coming upon his mother's body, cut to shreds and stripped of nearly every part of her so the humans could profit from it.

"Hello, Cooper. My goodness, you're even more

175

handsome than your father was. I never got a chance to ask you the other day, but do you enjoy being a human?" He told her that he did, and being a dragon as well. "Yes, I can well imagine that you'd like your other half more now that you have a mate. And she's breeding too. You must be very happy."

"I am. I don't want to be rude, but—"

"But he will be." Cooper felt his face heat up when Carson finished his statement for him. "Hello, Sadie. If I haven't told you this before, I'm so glad that made it so that Cooper was here for me when I needed him."

"Oh, how lovely of you to say that. Thank you." She looked at him, then back at Carson. "He has a right to be rude. I was the reason his father perished the way he did. But had he not, as you have said, his sons would never have made it this far."

"So you say." Sadie said nothing but sat when Carson asked her to. His brothers started to arrive one at a time. With his temper already not in a good place, he had to bite his tongue not to snap at them for being late. For Winnie—he didn't look at her. She still scared him a great deal. "Now, if we could begin, we'll have a reason for you to be here on our mountain."

"The mountain was the only place that I could go when I helped your father. I used all my magic, and even the dragons that were gathered there, to make sure that each of you got enough to be able to change. I've been resting, or hiding out, you could say, for a thousand years, give or take. Then when I woke, I watched over you all, just as I was asked to." Cooper asked how his dad using magic had drained her. "You don't think that he could have changed six full grown dragons into men without a little help, do you? Then there was the fact that you all had to be able to change back to dragons when you wished. No, your father was strong, but not that much."

"I don't believe you." Sadie said that was all right as well. "Are you admitting that you had a hand in my father's death?"

"Yes. But he knew what was going to happen well before I gave him as much as he could handle. Even as the king of dragons, your father could hold only so much magic. That's the reason we had to do it on the night of the meeting. Where all the dragons and their magic could be drawn from at once. I willed all that I was to him and took from each of the others until there was nearly enough. Had it not been for the lady of the faeries, I'm afraid that it would have failed. This your father knew as well." He asked why he'd not been told. "Would you have believed me, Cooper? I think not. Even had you hung around, which would have been a bad idea after you were changed, you would have noticed the weakened state of all the others there. You and your brothers meant that much to Coop that he'd willingly die to keep you safe."

"He was all we had left after mother was murdered, and you took him from us." No one said a word. He'd been loud and cruel. Not to mention, he felt sort of childish. "I'm sorry. I must have been holding that in for a long time."

"I have something for you from him. He knew he wasn't going to be around to give it to you when you were old enough to receive it. I have some of your mother's things as well. After you left the area, I had the faeries collect as much of them as they could find. I'm sorry there wasn't more, but

177

they did the best they could." He told her how Dad had said to burn what they couldn't carry when they left. "Yes, so the humans would never find you. Even then they had ways to track dragons that would mean their certain death. But the key I gave you before goes to the trunk that your father put things in for you. Items he managed to bring me to hide away for you all."

Sadie got up, and that was when he noticed how weak she was. It wasn't just her magic, but her body too was starting to show her age. When she made to carry a larger bag than she'd given to Carson, he got up and brought it over to the fireplace where they were all sitting. He even gave her his chair so that she might be warmer.

"You are weak." She said that she was beginning to show her age now as well. "You're going to die."

"Oh yes, and I'm ready to go. I've only been here this long because I made a promise to my best friend. And your father was the best a person could have asked for. He was forever finding me herbs that I didn't have. Making a mental list of things he knew I was short on. Once, he traveled all the way to the town to steal me a dress from the clothesline of a woman. You see, I had burnt mine while making a salve for your knee. You cut it running from a human, I believe."

"I remember that. I still have the scar from it." He smiled at the memory. "It stunk, if I recall correctly, and I told Dad that you had made it smell that bad just to be mean."

"I did, as a matter of fact. But it wasn't to be mean. It was all I could think to do when you were forever going to the town to see the children playing on the swings. And you might have been caught, had I not done that for you."

He nodded. "You were the most curious dragon I had ever encountered. Still are, I bet."

More memories were coming back to him with each passing minute and every item that they took from the bag. His brothers seemed to be remembering too, and told where they had come from and which one of them had given it to their mom.

"This is the shell we found when Mom took us to the lake beside the mountain. We couldn't be too loud because the humans were lurking everywhere." Hudson held it up as he continued. "She told me to bring something back that would remind me of the time we had fun. While we were in the water, I never thought once of the humans."

"That was more than likely the point, don't you think?" Hudson smiled and nodded. Sadie looked at Cooper when she spoke again. "There was some that I was sure that was part of a chess set. You learned it once, before all the madness of humans hunting you down. We got some of the pieces, but not all. You and your father played, didn't you?"

"Yes. He was never any good at it—the pieces and how they moved confused him. But we had so much fun learning it together. He said it was a good game to learn how to think one or two jumps ahead of the competition. I guess he was right, it did serve me well." He looked at Sadie as she closed her eyes and rocked with a smile on her face. "I'm truly sorry for the way I've spoken to you and treated you. You should have bashed me over the head and made me listen to you."

"Winnie said that she'd do it for me, but I told her that I didn't want you addled too much." She didn't open her eyes as she continued. "You used to have the hardest head when it came to teaching you something. It always had to be tried several different ways before you were satisfied with the one to make something work."

"He's still like that to this day." They all laughed, and Tristan told how the new contracts had to be gone over fifty times to make sure there were no loopholes. "Took me nearly a year to get them good enough where he'd sign off on them. And still he wasn't satisfied."

Each of them had a story to tell about when they were younger. Mostly it was the older ones. Xavier was the youngest, and by the time he was old enough to enjoy being a dragon, the humans had already invaded their camps and caves. But he did tell of the memories he had of their parents.

Cooper looked at Sadie again. "I'm ready for that trunk to be opened now. I think that I've grown up over the last few minutes. Thank you for that." She kissed him on the cheek and he felt the warmth of her, also her weakness. Being here was taking a great deal out of her. "If you'd like to rest, I'm sure that we can all wait on this."

"I cannot. I'm set to die this night, and your Winnie there has made me a few promises that I shall see if she does." He laughed when she did. "I am very old, Cooper. A strong witch that needs to rest forever now. It's been coming on more and more, and should I wait on this, I fear that I will not make it here a second time."

He nodded as the large container appeared in front of him. "When did he give this to you? He must have been preparing for this for months."

"Oh yes, for at least that long, if not longer. And your mother too. The plan had been to change you boys and they would remain as dragons. It would have worked too, as strong as your mother was. But she was murdered, as you know. So, some of the things in that are from her as well. A few I collected for them, being as how I look the part of being human. You'll be surprised at how much they cared for you all." Cooper nodded, almost afraid to open the container. "You'll be happy to know that your uncle put one or two items in there for you as well. He knew, you see, that your father was going to do this. And the night that he killed himself, he came to me and asked if he were to stay alive long enough for it to happen, would it make a difference. It did. His power, while not as strong as your father's, was still very helpful."

"How did uncle do it? I knew that he was unhappy, but how did he end his own life?" She told Lucas when he asked. "Threw himself over a cliff? How sad for him."

"Nay, he was flying, he told me before he left. He would do it once more before he hit the earth. He did it this way so that his body wouldn't be found for a long time. I don't think anyone ever disturbed his resting place but me. I had the faeries gather as much of him as was left, and we put him with his lovely wife and children. He is at peace now." Lucas thanked her. "No reason for that, my son. He was a good man too."

Lifting the lid off, Cooper noticed that it was padded with leather. The strings on the side, worn now, were also. He wondered at the hand that had crafted such a beautiful and sturdy box and thought to ask her later. As soon as he moved some of the heavy cloth out of the way, his breath caught at what he uncovered.

There on the top was the crown that his father had worn.

It was beaten silver, the jewel on it the purest diamond. Someone had carved a neat hole in the silver for the diamond to lay flat against it. There were no other adornments. His mother's, made with the same kind of silver and a single diamond, lay beneath his father's, and he felt his eyes well with tears when he touched his finger over hers.

"She was so proud of this. Told me when I was older that my mate would wear it proudly, and everyone would know that she was the queen of all dragons." He wiped at the tears that fell freely now. "Dad said that to have been given the honor of being king was the greatest thing he'd ever had. And having this crown to wear, it made him feel more than king. I thought them lost when they died."

He handed them around, letting everyone in the room have a chance to put them upon their head. Cooper laughed when it fell to the shoulders of his son and knew that someday he'd give it to him as his oldest.

Cooper was almost afraid to touch the next item, or even to reveal it. As he pulled away the cloth, he thought of his parents and how much they had given him. Then he saw the emeralds that had been theirs.

"Tears made from love will be the purest of emeralds. And once it is planted by another dragon in love, it will grow the most beautiful tree once they give it a part of themselves." Instead of finishing the saying, he passed the smaller of the two to Carson and showed his brothers the other. "When we're finished here, I'd like us to plant these. They'll bear fruit that will have emeralds in them once every sixty years."

"How very romantic." He kissed Carson and put his hand over their child. It was all he could do not to lean down and kiss his daughter as well. "I love you, Cooper."

"And I love you both. So very much." He held the container in his hand while he dug to the next layer. "Oh my. Oh, my good Lord."

~~~

Lincoln wasn't sure what he was looking at. It was tattered and old, that much he knew, but what it was he didn't have a clue. When the next item was handed to him, he held onto it and the one he'd had first.

"What is this?" Sadie wasn't looking well, and he figured this was her last business before she died. But he needed to know what these things were and what they meant to him and his brothers. "I mean, I can tell it's cloth, but other than that, I don't know."

"When your mother had to carry you from one place to the other, she would use that to tie the egg in and put it in her mouth. Sort of like the stork did in all those cartoons I've seen." Sadie laughed, then coughed hard. "That was used for all of you. She would tote you around like it was nothing so that she could fly with her mate. No other female did that but instead stayed hidden until the egg would hatch."

He looked at it with new eyes. His mother was very inventive and special. He passed it to his brother and held up the next piece. Lincoln had a feeling that he knew what it was but needed to be sure. If it was what he thought, it was more precious than gold to him.

"Your mother's scale. When the faeries were looking for something to bring back to my resting place, they found that. Sadly, it was the only piece of her that was left. I'm sorry. The other is your father's. Since he died in one piece, he was buried with your mother's bones and a tooth that they also found." He nodded, touched that the faeries were so kind to them. "They lie side by side, the two of them. When you are finished here, I shall tell you where to find them."

"Thank you, I'd like that." He handed his father's scale to Grace. When she held it in her hand, she looked so much smaller with it there. When she passed it on to someone else, he wondered if she knew what having them would mean. It was a piece of the last of their kind. The last fully dragon king and queen.

There were other things in the box, nothing so important to him as the scales. As the other pieces were passed around, he kept coming back to the necklace that had startled Cooper so much when he'd found it. It was a diamond as large as his fist, and uncut. It would be worth billions. Their mother had left instructions on what to do with it.

She wanted a college fund set up for the underprivileged children of the town where they lived. He supposed she'd never thought that they'd stay so close to where they had perished, but none of them could leave their home.

The money from the sale of the diamond would pay full tuition for both male and female humans that had lost their parents to some sort of accident or sudden death. It was something that they were already doing, in the name of Molly Conrad. He'd have to talk to Cooper and the others about what they could do now. Add to the foundation or set up a second? These were things that they would work out.

The gifts from their uncle were funny. He had thought of himself as an artist. Carving into wood with his claws, he would create the most hideous things with them. But they all thought that to tell him would hurt his feelings. So, he sent each of them a piece that he'd made. It was touching as well.

The last item had been pulled out when Sadie stood. They thought she was leaving.

"Nay, I have one more gift to give you all. It's magic." Cooper said that he thought they had plenty and suggested that she keep it to make herself well. "You are a kind young man, Cooper, but I cannot use what isn't mine. This was for you all, and when the rest of you have mates, it will come to them as well. This is the magic that your father couldn't give you when he changed you. That of true immortality."

"What do you mean, true immortality? We're that now, aren't we?" Lincoln looked around when the rest of them agreed with him. "What's different about this magic?"

"You will no longer have to fear a pierce to the heart. No one will be able to remove your head. Nor will iron make you ill or kill you. You will be able to walk among the humans and never fear that they'll harm you again." Cooper looked at Lincoln when he cursed. "Yes, that's what I said when I figured out that it wouldn't be passed the way the other had been. This requires a witch to touch you and to take one thing from you that you are willing to give. A drop of blood will be enough."

"But you'll have some of the magic, won't you? I mean, we've only just gotten to know you. Again, I should say, but you have so many stories to tell us about our parents." She looked at Cooper and put her fingers to his forehead. When he fell back, Carson stood and demanded to know what she'd done to him. "It's all right. She gave me her memories. All of them. I know everything she does." Carson sat, but she didn't

185

seem happy about this turn of events.

After Sadie sat down again, she asked them each for the drop of blood. Cooper was to go last, for he was to get more of the magic than they were getting. What it would be was a mystery, but Lincoln was glad that the women would be included. He never had to worry about Grace again.

When his turn came, he stood before her, then went to his knees so that she could reach him. She was getting weaker still, and he worried that she'd not make it to her garden that she'd told them had been prepared. Sadie touched him on the cheeks and smiled at him before speaking.

"Your mother loved you all so very much, and I felt her heart when she was murdered. All she could think about was her babies, and who was going to take them on walks and play with them in the sky as she'd done for you." He nodded, feeling his eyes fill as hers were. "The night she was killed, do you remember the date?"

"My birthday. I turned one hundred that day." Sadie nodded. "I've never celebrated any since that night. It would make me think of her, and it would break my heart all over again."

"You should celebrate them again, young Lincoln. Her last thoughts were of you, and how you would only remember that she died that day and not that you would be growing into a man. She feared, you see, that you'd only feel her pain and suffering. That she did not want for you. For her, I would like you to celebrate your birth. It is what she would have wanted." He nodded, sobbing now that she would think of him while dying. "There's a good boy. Now, I want you to think of me when you have your cake. It is something that I loved more than I did my teas."

A burst of laughter fell from his lips, and he smiled at her through his tears. "I promise to eat a piece in your honor, Sadie."

When he moved on so that his brothers could give her some of their blood, he thought of his mother and how much he missed her. She was taken too soon, and they were too young to have lost someone so dear to their hearts. Then not a month later, their father had died as well.

Lincoln felt the magic when it rolled over them. Grace, who was sitting on his lap now, moaned as it settled over her as well. And when Sadie stood and gave the little more to Cooper, she fell into the chair again and closed her eyes.

"It is time, I believe. I shall go to my death with an unburdened heart. But a full one. I will forever, no matter that I am gone from this world, remember you boys and all that you have done for your family. Thank you for seeing an old woman."

When she closed her mouth, they all knew that she had taken her last breath. Sadie the Golden Witch of the mountain, was no more.

The faeries and brownies showed up just after she had passed. They took her body out of the house, and he was reminded of when his father had passed as well. Lincoln decided that he'd visit their gardens soon. And Sadie's as well. He might even take her a piece of his cake on his birthday and share it with her. It was the least he could do for someone who had come on her death bed to give them their parents back. And that's what it felt like. That she'd brought them back a moment in time of the people that had given up everything for them. Their lives included. Lincoln would remember this, and the memories that she'd brought to them, to tell his children about a witch and a pair of blue dragons.

Chapter 13

Grace held her son in her arms as the rest of the family ate dinner. They were just as loud as they usually were, but the cursing had stopped. She was glad for it.

The other day Mattie had been staying with them and said she'd dropped her fucking milk. The glass had shattered, of course, but it was the way she'd said it that had shocked her to the core. After that, she had a talk with everyone, and told them to curb it or be thrown to the curb. They got the message loud and clear.

"You want me to take him?" She handed Bradley to Lincoln and was amazed someone as large as he was could be so gentle with such a small thing. And get the baby to sleep faster than she could at bedtime as well.

When she got up to get another drink, she caught her sister and Mark necking in the hallway. Clearing her throat to warn them only made Ginger jump. Mark, however, laughed at being discovered.

"We're happy, what can I say?" She told him it showed in them both. "It feels good to be in love, don't you think, Grace? And I have children too. A little boy and the most wonderful girl."

He'd told Ginger that it mattered little to him who their father was. All he wanted was raise them with her, and hope they turned out for the best. Grace didn't see them being anything but well-loved children, and they were already talking about having more. Ginger had never had a planned pregnancy, and she was really looking forward to having it with Mark, she told her.

"Before I forget to tell you, we're going to move into the Conrad house now that it's empty of all that stuff. That way we'll be closer to you guys. Mark is having someone repaint all the walls too." They'd been living in a rental since they'd been together. She missed her sister sometimes but was glad she was happy. She deserved it.

Looking out the kitchen window as she drank her tea, she thought about the paintings out there. The ones that she'd been working on for two weeks now. Deciding that no one would miss her — and if they did, they knew where she'd be — she went out to the studio and pulled the sheet off the large painting, so that she could work on it. It was nearly done, and with the others, there were a total of twelve. She thought it was her best work yet.

It was during the nineteen thirties, and her muse had lived in one of the places along the docks. To have called it an apartment would have grossly over stated what it was. It was four walls that had running water only when it rained. And even then, it would have been left from the tenant above her.

The large painting was of the apartment. The three-legged table sat in the very middle of the room. There wasn't a chair to be had, so she used an old crate to sit on. It also served as extra storage space if needed. Muse couldn't read or write, but she could sing. It would make her a coin or two when she was able to get off work early enough to literally sing for her supper. Her money packet would go for rent and what little food she could afford. Which wasn't all that much.

The rats in the corners were to show how bad it had been for her. Her coarse laughter belied the sound of her voice when she was singing. There was a picture on the wall, torn from a newspaper long ago. It had been tacked up by a nail that had seen better days.

Her dress was washed every other day, and now it hung near the window that wasn't open but provided a nice breeze because the glass had been broken. She sat in her shift, her boots drying by the door so the rats wouldn't chew through them again.

She sat on her crate eating a rotten potato, the last of her food until she got her pay packet again next week. Unlike the other muses that she'd worked with, this one spoke to her as she painted and brought what she was telling her to life. It was why it seemed so real—she had someone telling her just exactly what she needed it to look like, so that her story could be told.

Lincoln joined her just as she was cleaning her brushes. The painting was finished; they all were. As he stood in front of it, looking at it with fresh eyes, she asked what he thought about it.

"It looks wonderful. You've got so much detail in it that

you can almost smell the potato she's eating. And the way that you gave the viewer the entire room, it says a lot for her living conditions. Did she ever tell you her name?" She told him that none of them except for Hank's father knew them. "That's so sad. But I don't think anyone would recognize her. You've turned her face just enough so that you only see her sunken cheeks. She looks starved."

"She was. That's how she died, she told me. A few days after this point in the painting, she was found lying on her sheets. They just wrapped her up in them and threw her in the rubbish bin. There is a painting in the other room that reflects that. But you'd have to remember the color of the sheet in this one to get it." He nodded. "She's gone now. She left when she said that it was perfect. I hope Garrett will take these. They're a little darker than the others were."

"He will. He's been trying to get me to tell him what muse is working with you now. I think he's right in calling your art The Muse Painter." She liked it as well. "Do you have anyone wanting you now? Or are they giving you a break?"

"I have someone, but he wants to wait a little while. He can see me with the baby, and that makes him very happy." Lincoln pulled her into his arms. "The others must think I'm rude, just walking away like that."

"No, they know how your mind works now. Even Cooper said you'd need a break from this one soon. He knows as well as I do that you've been out here a great deal." She looked up at him and smiled. "I don't like that. It means I'm going to have to do something I won't be thrilled about, doesn't it?"

"I want to have a big country Christmas. I know it's a few months away, but I want to plan for it now." He said that he'd like that as well. "I don't have a lick of ornaments, nor do we have the first thing for Bradley."

"I'm sure that he won't remember this Christmas any more than Wendall will. They're too young to care." She told him that she would. "Of course. All right, we'll start looking for ornaments. I know this really nice Christmas shop that we can go to and get a start. How big of a tree are you thinking?"

"One that will fill the corner in the living room. And another for the entrance hall. That way everyone can see it as soon as they come in." He told her that was a good idea. "Also, I want to paint all of you around it. For the mantel."

"As in the women too?" She said that was it. And when the others came, she'd add them in. "Okay, that sounds good. And I like the fact that you're so positive there will be more. Why are you so sure?"

"The fates would want all of you to be happy. Don't you think?" Lincoln nodded, but didn't look convinced. "My sister even got a nice man out of this. The dragons are bringing their mates to see you guys, and the sooner the better if you ask me."

"Tristan is terrified of his mate. He hasn't met her yet, and he's afraid that she's going to be a ball buster, and he won't be able to handle that." She laughed with him. "I told him she could be a gentle soul too and do whatever he wants. I think that frightened him too. He wants to have fun. I guess we'll see when she gets here."

They talked about the mates coming while she cleaned up. Grace would need to call Garrett in the morning so he could finally see the paintings. She'd gotten into the habit of not allowing him to until they were all finished. He tended to drive her batty asking how far she was from completing the next one, so he could see it. She got more work done that way.

They sat in the living room and she rocked Bradley while he took his late bottle. He was a good boy, sleeping through the night and only waking up if he was too wet. Rarely did that happen, and she was glad. As a new mom, she was getting much more sleep than Ginger.

After he was taken up to bed by the nanny, she sat on the couch with Lincoln. She was making a list of things she wanted to get for Christmas to make the house shine, and he was reading the paper. It was what they did nightly to relax after a long day.

When he woke her up, she realized that she must have dozed off and he'd carried her up to their room. Lincoln even undressed her and put her in the bed. She told him that she was exhausted.

"You no longer have Muse keeping you awake all night, wanting you to paint." She nodded and closed her eyes. "You rest now, love, and I'll see you in the morning."

~~~

Lucas stood in line at the bank. He had to make several deposits, and didn't want to be rushed about it. Sometimes when he came in this late there would be someone behind him, huffing and puffing about how long he was taking. He told Ginger he'd do it today since he was leaving the office early.

He was two from the teller when he heard the man yelling from the front of the bank. Robbery? Today? Damn it. His first afternoon off in a month, and now he had to deal with this crap. Sitting on the floor where he was told, Lucas reached out to his brothers and told them what was going on. Cooper laughed, and Xavier said to shift and step on him. He had such funny brothers. But they did promise to call the police.

The man is a bear shifter, and he has a hint of tiger on him. No, not that, something more domestic. A cat, maybe? I don't know. Anyway, he has two guns in his hands, as well as one on his ankle. You know, for a bank this size, you'd think he'd have a partner or two. Carson pointed out that he was a shifter robbing a bank with other shifters inside; he couldn't be too terribly smart. *True. But this is seriously messing with my plans tonight. I was going to order a pizza and eat it in front of the television.*

Isn't that what you do every night? He was going to hit them all when he got out of here. Lincoln went on with his teasing. *The last time I went by your house and it was trash day, I think I counted like fifteen empty pizza boxes.*

Very funny. You should go on the road. You could be a comedy act all by yourself. It'll take away from that when I disfigure you. Lucas told them what was going on now. *He wants the bank manager. Something about being turned down for a loan here. He's losing his house too.*

Do you know who it is yet? He said that he didn't, the man was wearing a mask. *I've been asked if he's limping.* Cooper explained how he was in town on an errand and had come to the bank when he'd called out. The police were there now, and they were trying to get the man to answer the phone.

Yes, he's limping. He's got the bank manager down on his knees now. I think he means to kill him. Lucas stood. He didn't want anyone killed if he could help it, and the man screamed at him to sit down. "Look, I know that you're upset, but killing that man isn't going to help your situation."

195

"You think not? It'll certainly make me feel better knowing that he's dead." Lucas asked if he could help him secure a loan. "You got money you can hand over without asking for my firstborn? I felt like he was going to when I was here last week."

"I'm sorry that he put you through that, but the truth of the matter is, he was just doing his job. The people higher than him are the ones that make him follow the rules. And then there are more above them that do the same. It's a nightmare." The man nodded and seemed to have relaxed his finger off the trigger. "Why don't you put the gun down, and perhaps you and I can work something out?"

"You're one of them Manning people, aren't you?" Lucas told him his name. "Yeah, that's it. My sister works for one of the million companies that you own. You've been bringing jobs around."

"We're trying. Do you need a job?" He said that he couldn't work due to his medical record. "Why is that?"

"I've got something wrong with my head. Sometimes I don't know where I am or how I got there." Lucas asked if he meant he was blacking out. "Yeah. I told the doctor down at the veteran's place, and they said it was all in my head. Ain't that what I was saying to him? Anyway, he gave me medicine, but it costs so much. This guy wouldn't give me a loan against my house so I could buy it, see?"

"Okay, put down the gun and I'll work something out with you to buy your drugs." He said it wouldn't work. "Why not? You don't want to take your meds?"

"It's too late for that."

The gun went off and Lucas fell back.

He knew on some level he was hurt, but his mind was still trying to work around that he'd been shot. When the second sounded, he knew that the man, whoever he was, had either shot himself or the bank manager. Either way, he wasn't going to loan him the money now. Someone slapped him in the face and he looked up at Winnie.

"I've been hurt." She said no shit or I'm sorry, but he was reasonably sure, knowing her, it was the former. "He shot me, and I think I'm going to be sick."

"You puke on me and I'll make you hurt worse than you are right now." He said that he really did hurt. "I know. I've got you now. We're going to take you to the hospital. Okay?"

That wasn't right. Winnie had turned into Carson, and he wasn't sure where Winnie had gone. Then he saw Cooper, who was yelling at him. Something about him not being able to die and he'd better not be testing the theory. Closing his eyes, he tried to make the room stop spinning, but all that did was make him sicker. Things were not going well for him.

The next few times he opened his eyes, he quickly shut them again. Things were moving. The walls were swaying back and forth. His hands were invisible. And he couldn't feel his fingers. When he asked someone for a trash can, he could have sworn he was going to be sick, but all he did was heave. Then nothing.

"Mr. Manning? Can you hear me?" He opened one eye. That was all he could manage with the other being held down. "Mr. Manning, my name is Doctor Carver. I'm the one that operated on you."

"You're very pretty." She thanked him, but he could tell he annoyed her. "What happened to me?"

"You were shot. Do you remember anything about it?" He wasn't sure what was real or not, and told her about Winnie turning into Carson, and then his brother telling him he ate fifteen boxes of pizza. "I don't know what that means, but I've removed the bullets. I'm to understand you're a dragon. Can you shift and heal?"

"I'm not sure there's enough room in here." She looked around, but it was too much for him and he closed his eyes. She asked him to please open them and look at her. "You smell pretty too. Almost like almonds and vanilla. Do you wear that?"

"No, I don't wear perfume. Can you tell me your name?" He sang the little song about pudding and tang or something like that, and she frowned at him. "Mr. Manning, did you hit your head too?"

"You're her, aren't you?" She asked who that would be. "The one. The other half. The one and only for Lucas Manning."

He was singing again and felt silly when he realized it. Trying to straighten up, he looked at her once more. She was asking him to tell her his name, and he couldn't remember anything but how she smelled. And how beautiful she was. She asked again if he'd hit his head.

"I don't know. Maybe when I fell back." He looked at her, everything coming to him in that second. "I was shot. He shot me in the chest and I fell back. Did he kill the bank manager?"

"Yes, then himself. The other customers said you tried to get him to not kill anyone." He said he had. "Are you stupid? What the hell were you thinking, bargaining with a man with a gun? Christ, men are so stupid."

"Even pissed off, I think you're lovely."

He felt a pinch in his arm, then he began to fade out. The doctor told him not to fight it, and he promised that he wouldn't, that he was happy with her. If she said anything else, Lucas didn't remember it.

Before You Go...

HELP AN AUTHOR

write a review

THANK YOU!

Share your voice and help guide other readers to these wonderful books. Even if it's only a line or two your reviews help readers discover the author's books so they can continue creating stories that you'll love. Login to your favorite retailer and leave a review. Thank you.

AWARD WINNING, BESTSELLING AUTHOR

Kathi Barton, winner of the Pinnacle Book Achievement award as well as a best-selling author on Amazon and All Romance books, lives in Nashport, Ohio with her husband Paul. When not creating new worlds and romance, Kathi and her husband enjoy camping and going to auctions. She can also be seen at county fairs with her husband who is an artist and potter.

Her muse, a cross between Jimmy Stewart and Hugh Jackman, brings her stories to life for her readers in a way that has them coming back time and again for more. Her favorite genre is paranormal romance with a great deal of spice. You can visit Kathi online and drop her an email if you'd like. She loves hearing from her fans. aaronskiss@gmail.com.

Follow Kathi on her blog: http://kathisbartonauthor. blogspot.com/